A blazing new combat novel based on ABC-TV's exciting action adventure series—one of America's most popular weekly TV shows.

THE RAT PATROL #6
in
Desert Masquerade

Getting behind the Jerries' lines is comparatively easy for the Rat Patrol. Masquerading as Italian gangsters with information to sell Dietrich, they have no trouble at all getting into the Jerry camp. Once there they are able to quickly discover the location of the German land mines.

But getting out again without arousing the Germans' suspicions becomes a problem for Troy, Tully, Hitch and Moffitt. They know their information—vital to the newest Allied offensive—is useless unless they can get it to Wilson. To make matters more desperate, they know that within a few hours the Allies will be bombing the camp and the entire surrounding area.

Trapped behind enemy lines, they wonder if this is fated to be the Rat Patrol's final caper.

THE RAT PATROL

#6 in Desert Masquerade

by David King

PAPERBACK LIBRARY, Inc.

New York

PAPERBACK LIBRARY EDITION

First Printing: June, 1968

*Paperback Library books are published by Paperback Library, Inc.
Its trademark, consisting of the words "Paperback Library" ac-
companied by an open book, is registered in the United States
Patent Office.* Paperback Library, Inc., 315 Park Avenue South,
New York, N.Y. 10010.

1

The bombardment at dawn shook Colonel Dan Wilson from his cot. Wearily the tight-faced commander of the Allied armored column stumbled across the sand floor of the HQ tent and stood at the opened flap watching the red-white bursts that ignited the ashen sky. The whoosh and thunder of the shells from the ridge seemed more intense this morning than usual. Vivid flames streaked across the flannel-colored sky that had just begun to lighten. The desert shuddered and belched hot sand. He glanced swiftly from left to right. In slit trenches along and behind a dozen halftracks dispersed in a wide-angled V a hundred yards in front of him, only a few men were stirring. Most slept on, unmindful of the rock-ridged hill several miles away that bloomed with muzzle flame and echoed the pounding of artillery. No more than they any longer awakened at the parachuted flares that showered the nights with light.

The situation was impossible, Wilson thought angrily. That was Jerry up there on the ridge throwing thunder and lightning at Wilson's column and he couldn't do a thing about it. Not that the enemy was achieving anything with his flares and artillery except to assure himself that the Allies hadn't tossed caution to the wind and sent the armor charging at the position. Wilson had tried it once. He would not again until he knew a great deal more than he now did.

Across and well above the sandy floor of the tawny desert, Hauptmann Hans Dietrich of the Afrika Korps was secure in his strategic position. A spiney thrust of rock jutted northward toward the sea. To the south the ridge dropped into a salt marsh that glittered for fifty impassable miles. Dietrich held the pass and could not be flanked.

Dietrich had been beaten and battered at his own stronghold of Sidi Abd deep in the Libyan desert. He had fled up through the swirling sands with the Allied armor pounding hard on the clanking treads of the Jerry column. Scarcely pausing to refill with gasoline and water, Wilson had denied Dietrich any opportunity to regroup to make a stand or maneuver to flank. It had not been an orderly withdrawal for Dietrich. The Jerries had been routed and the uncharted desert had been strewn with the shredded remnants of Dietrich's might—Jerry armor and vehicles discarded when they could push ahead no longer, Wilson remembered bitterly. Exhausted and unable to continue running, the Jerry column had sprawled at last within grasp on the ridge. Or so Wilson had thought.

Dietrich had nearly trapped Wilson here. Precipitous as the flight had been, it had not been aimless. Wilson grimly admitted that Dietrich had led him into this well-fortified position. The sloping approach to the ridge was heavily mined and backed by a ledge of mortars. Infantry and machine gun positions were burrowed in horizontal shelves above and gun emplacements of 75s and rocket launchers were dug in at the top. Trying to take such a fixed position with tanks would be murder.

He'd very nearly been caught in the trap, Wilson thought with slow, burning resentment as the Jerry shells continued to shriek across the sands in the early morning. He'd watched Dietrich's Mark IVs lumber up the grade through the pass no more than half an hour ahead, and he'd sent a flying wedge, a V of a dozen Shermans, in hot pursuit. The hill and the ridge had been quiet as the tanks moved up with his close friend, Major Gus Runstead, tank commander, on the point. The Shermans ground toward the foot of the slope unchallenged, and Runstead's tank started up the grade with the others fanned out. An explosion erupted on the grade over which the Mark IVs had passed only half an hour earlier. Runstead's tank shuddered to a canting halt, its right tread blown. The grade and slope had been mined, and the Jerries, undetected, had used a safe passage through the field. To the left of Runstead's tank, a second Sherman struck a mine, plunged forward on its nose

6

and burst into flame. From above, mortars began lobbing shells at the cripples and the 75s on top opened direct fire on the phalanx. Runstead's tank took an armor-piercing shell through its bowels and exploded. Far to the right, a third Sherman went up in a blast of smoke and fire. The Shermans raked the hillside with their 75s but could not dig out the enemy nor withstand his barrage. Wilson had withdrawn his assault force, but not before another Sherman had been put out of action.

Dietrich's flight had ended on the ridge. His tanks were up there, supplementing the emplaced artillery, ready to pounce when the Jerry column had regained its strength. It infuriated Wilson. He was impotent. He had withdrawn his own armor on the barren sand sea beyond the reach of the enemy.

First, Wilson had a V of Shermans a hundred yards apart but ready to converge in formation—thirty Sherman medium tanks with 75 mm. cannon and .30 caliber machine guns. The five-man crews were on alert in slit trenches beside their weapons. Then there were a dozen M-15 halftracks each mounting an automatic 37 mm. gun and two .50 caliber antiaircraft machine guns. Behind the halftracks was the communications van and his HQ tent. To the rear were dozens of supply trucks, which had multiplied until Wilson's position looked like a motor pool. They were in a vulnerable position and at the first indication that Dietrich was coming off the ridge to fight, he'd send them back to the base at Bir el Alam, a hundred and fifty miles to the southeast. Meanwhile he clung to the idea that somehow he'd find a way to crash through the fortifications. He'd need the trucks to cart the supplies if the column ever got Dietrich on the run again.

It enraged Wilson to think that for once he had supplies in sufficient quantity plus superior armored strength and could not engage the enemy. Actually the advantage was the enemy's. The situation was a standoff until Dietrich felt he was strong enough to come out in the open or chose to withdraw his armor with his rear protected at the ridge to the main force of the Afrika Korps, which was engaged with the British Eighth Army somewhere near Tunisia.

Until now Dietrich appeared to be licking his wounds and waiting. Wilson occasionally was permitted the use of a light observation plane, which flew in from the base at Bir el Alam. It would land on a strip which had been smoothed on the desert by hand. Hopefully, and to give the men something to do, the strip, located behind the supply trucks, had been extended until it was long enough to take a B-25 medium bomber. The observation plane would refuel and circle the ridge beyond the reach of the 75s. A few bombers over the ridge would have been more useful, but Wilson had been told they could not be spared for this action. Maybe a containing action here was all that was necessary in this campaign, Wilson thought angrily, but the trouble was that it was he who was being contained.

Much more frequently than Wilson was permitted the use of the observation craft, Dietrich managed to get two ME-109s, probably from Tunis. The square-wingtipped fighters would swoop over the ridge with their 20 mm. cannon hammering. Although Wilson's .50 caliber antiaircraft machine guns had yet to score a kill, the concentrated fire from the halftracks did drive the Messerschmitts far enough upstairs so that to date the only casualties from their forays had been the canvas top of one truck and a water barrel.

It was, Wilson thought as the sun began to touch the sky with blue and gold, a hell of a way to fight a war. A barrage of mortar shells cratered the desert more than a mile away and the ridge went quiet. Time out for breakfast, he thought with sardonic humor. Jerry probably would remain unprotesting until the sudden desert dusk dropped over this strange battlefield.

He watched as his men began to crawl from their holes, shredding waxed containers from rations to build small fires. They'd heat water for powdered coffee, prepare powdered eggs and heat some potted meat. Breakfast in the lingering cool of morning was the one hot meal they ate. The rest of the day they sought what little shade their vehicles afforded, moving with the sun and sweating it out. A stinking way to fight a war, he repeated to himself, turning back into the tent as he saw his first sergeant, Dewey Peilowski, shambling toward HQ.

The tank crews were growing flabby-minded with inactivity, he thought as he washed in a metal basin on a wooden crate and pulled on battle fatigues. At first they'd been enraged that Dietrich had turned a trick on them, but now they no longer seemed to care. The desert was like that. Unless you were fighting for your life, it sapped your will to win. Even Peilowski was going to pot. He'd begged to come along, see some action, bang off some shells. He'd been tired of HQ and wanted to flex his muscles with the men. Now since they'd been here on this desert flat, tough old Army man Peilowski had voluntarily taken on the duties of an orderly. Just to have something to do.

Peilowski bumbled into the tent. Already his fair but sunburned face was sweaty and his blue eyes were dull. He brought in a can of warm water for Wilson's morning shave, nodded and stepped just outside the tent to prepare breakfast for both of them. It made Wilson sick.

"Another day of the same," Peilowski said heavily as he handed Wilson a canteen cup of tepid coffee and wiped his forehead with the back of his hand. "This is one time I guess even the Rat Patrol can't help."

"I'm afraid you guess right," Wilson snapped. Either you gave way to torpor or your temper got short.

Wilson's temper was short when the Rat Patrol was mentioned. They were his four-man army. Sergeants Sam Troy and Jack Moffitt and Privates Mark Hitchcock and Tully Pettigrew were undisciplined mavericks who wrote their own rules and conducted their own brand of warfare against the enemy. They were his long-range penetration commando group. With their two jeeps mounting .50 caliber machine guns and their unconventional assortment of weapons and explosives, they'd harassed Dietrich everywhere in the desert. He wasn't angry with them. He was enraged at this intolerable situation where he didn't dare use them.

He wanted to send them on a mission. If he knew the pattern of the minefield, the safe passage through it, the positions of the mortars and machine guns, the locations of the gun emplacements and the dispersement of the armor, he would risk a massed assault. It was the kind of mission they'd cheer. And once behind Dietrich's lines, they'd get the information. But Dietrich expected them. He was waiting for them. Even though they started from far behind the Allied position under cover of night, and whether they approached Jerry from land or sea or even dropped in from the sky, they'd find a reception committee. The Rat Patrol had been the weapon Wilson had used to defeat Dietrich on too many occasions, and Wilson wasn't going to risk losing them now.

Wilson tossed off his coffee, strapped his twin pearl-handled pistols about his waist and clapped the white enameled helmet with the golden eagle over his close-cropped gray hair. He bent from the hips to leave the tent, stood and braced his shoulders, ready to make the tedious morning tour of inspection. His jaw set at his own attitude. He hadn't realized the lethargy had reached him.

From the back of the communications van between the tent and the V of halftracks, Corporal John Locke, his carrot-topped radio operator, hopped down and trotted toward HQ. Wilson halted. There was urgency in Locke's movements, and moreover, Locke was on duty. It was unlike him to leave the Command Set. There were a dozen men within call from the van who could have brought the message Locke had folded in his fist.

"It came in security code," Locke said, standing as tall as Wilson himself. Wilson felt a tingle of excitement as he took the penciled message. Only Locke and himself—not even Peilowski or the executive officer at base—had access to the security code. Locke had been given special clearance. "I've decoded it and destroyed the original," he added.

The message was for Eyes Only. Locke watched closely as Wilson read it, automatically reached for his Zippo, lighted the paper and dropped it to the sand when the paper flamed. When Wilson had ground the charred bits into the ground, Locke turned and strolled back to the van.

The message which Wilson had destroyed to Locke's satisfaction had read: *New missile launcher designed for area saturation bombardment arriving with ordnance expert your position for testing within week. Prepare landing facilities for C-47. Utmost security and secrecy essential.*

Wilson turned swiftly back into the tent. His eyes were narrow and his lips were thin. His mind was chewing at the message. Peilowski already was at his typewriter, preparing to occupy himself during another day of duty with the tanks by battling with the forms.

10

"Get out a work detail," Wilson said abruptly. "Prepare the landingstrip for a C-47."

Peilowski's jaw slackened and he looked mutely at Wilson for a moment. "We already done it," he protested. "We fixed it for a B-25, it'll take a C-47."

"Do it again," Wilson growled. "Go over it foot by foot. Make sure it's smooth and packed."

"Yes, sir," Peilowski said, and a startled look leaped into his eyes.

Unmindful of his first sergeant's uncomprehending stare, Wilson sat on the edge of his cot, gray eyes half closed in concentration. He considered the wording and implication of the message: a new weapon, a missile launcher designed for area saturation bombardment. Since this would be a test, there probably would be only one, no more than two of the launchers at the most and a limited number of missiles. He wondered what the size and capabilities of the missiles would be, the area that could be hit with saturation bombardment. The main thing was to know the strategic target area. If he knew where to direct the test firing, this new weapon might provide a breakthrough and safe passage for his armor to the ridge. He could push his column through immediately following the firing and take Dietrich completely by surprise. It was an opportunity he could not afford to lose.

"Peilowski!" he barked at his thick-backed first sergeant, who was shuffling from the tent with his clipboard under his arm. "Right now, at once, before you round up that work detail, find Troy and send him to me. On the double. I think I have an assignment for the Rat Patrol."

Two hundred yards behind the HQ tent and two hundred yards in front of the rows of canvas topped supply trucks, four signs marked the corners of a splotchy tan patch on the sandy carpet of the desert. The signs read: OFF LIMITS. They marked the area covered by the camouflage nets which the Rat Patrol had spliced together and used to roof the hole they'd dug and into which they'd driven the jeeps. They were not particularly concerned with concealing the jeeps. In fact, they had them out in sight of the Jerries almost every day. The hidden hollow had merely given them an excuse to provide themselves with quarters that afforded some protection from the sun during the scorching days and shelter from the cold at night. The jeeps were parked well apart. In the ten feet that separated the deadly little vehicles with their big smashing weapons, Sergeants Sam Troy and Jack Moffitt and Privates Tully Pettigrew and Mark Hitchcock sprawled, each wrapped in a GI blanket, asleep and for the moment unaware of the war.

At the far end of the burrow, Hitch rolled over, sat up stretching, crawled to one of the jeeps, and pulled his red-topped French Foreign Legion cap from the front seat. He fished a piece of bubble gum from inside the cap, put it into his mouth, enclosed his face with steel-rimmed GI glasses, and clapped the black-billed cap on the back of his red-haired head. He was ready to face the day.

"Tully, you awake?" he asked quietly.

"Just on one side," the flat-cheeked Kentuckian drawled.

"Let's run out a jeep, drive to the ocean and have a swim," Hitch said in a whisper. "This place is beginning to bug me."

"You don't reckon Troy will have a catnip fit?" Tully asked softly, sitting up and digging in the pocket of his shirt for a matchstick. He put it between his teeth and rolled it to one side of his mouth.

At the other end of the cavern, Troy lay with his arms behind his head, studying without interest the patterns in the camouflage nets. "Why not?" Troy said without moving. "The Jerries are bound to see us take off. It should give them something to think about. Maybe stir them up. Maybe they'll send a patrol after us. Maybe we can get this war under way again."

"Splendid thought," Moffitt said with Cambridge in his voice. He'd been detached from the Scots Greys for special desert service with the Rat Patrol. He sat up and adjusted the dark beret on his head. There was a faintly amused smile on his lips. "We can all use some ablutionary activity."

"That isn't against regulations?" Hitch asked with mock concern in his voice.

"You know ablutions are against regulations," Troy said with a tight smile. He sat up with the others. "Otherwise you and Tully wouldn't be conspiring."

"My, my," Tully drawled.

"Do we tell the colonel we're taking off?" Hitch wanted to know.

"No!" Troy said sharply. He reached beside him for the Australian bush hat that was as much a part of his uniform as his boots. "He'd figure we were up to some kind of caper on our own and tell us to stay put."

"Then we'll be AWOL," Tully moaned in despair. "That'll be worse than abluting."

"Nuts," Hitch said, kneeling to roll his blanket. He tossed it in the back of the jeep he drove. "Let's tear down the ceiling and take off before Peilowski puts us on a detail policing up the area."

"Perhaps we can indulge in a spot of fishing," Moffitt said, stooping and crawling up the sand ramp at the end of the cavern. "I've always fancied kippers for breakfast."

"A fine thing," Troy said disgustedly, following Moffitt

13

up to the desert. "Breakfast on the beach. I never thought the Rat Patrol would come to this."

Troy looked toward the inactive halftracks and tanks where men still drowsed. It was like a rest camp. He was fed up with Wilson's do-nothing attitude. So Dietrich had them in a temporary bind. That Jerry hadn't stopped them yet. The thing to do was smash at him where he least expected it instead of sitting back and waiting for him to make the first move. The trouble with Wilson was he didn't have any imagination. Troy looked up toward the ridge where all seemed peaceful in the serene cool of the blue early morning. Wilson was playing the fool. Dietrich wasn't the type to sit quietly in a secure position. He was up to something and Wilson ought to know what it was. Instead of going to the ocean, the Rat Patrol should load the jeeps with charges and speed south around the salt marsh. If nothing else, at least they could create a diversion at the enemy's rear and in the resulting confusion Wilson's armor should be able to penetrate at some area.

Orders or not, it wasn't such a bad idea, he thought seriously as he picked up one corner of the camouflage net. At least it would get Wilson off his fat butt. Which wasn't exactly true, he admitted with a brief grin. The old man didn't have a fat butt. He was as lean and hard as a rail. It was his head that was fat.

"Troy!" His name was bellowed and he jerked his head toward the HQ tent. Peilowski was trotting toward him. Troy straightened and watched in amazement. Blubbery Peilowski never moved faster than a shamble. Peilowski was waving one arm excitedly and perspiration was running down his pink cheeks.

"The colonel wants you," he shouted before he had covered half the distance to the burrow. "Right now. Shake it, Troy, shake it."

"Now what do you imagine has buggered him?" Moffitt murmured.

"The old man had his ear to the ground," Hitch said irritably, dropping his corner of the net. "He heard we were going swimming."

"You know, you may be right," Troy said, strolling toward Peilowski. "What's up?" he asked the first sergeant.

"All I know is, he told me to drop everything and get

14

you," Peilowski said, grasping Troy's arm and tugging. "Move, man."

"Hands off," Troy said tightly, brushing off the hand. He turned to the others. "Better hang around. It might be a caper."

"Nuts," Hitch said, and pushed his cap to the back of his head. "He thinks we can't take care of ourselves any longer."

Perhaps Wilson finally did have something useful for the Rat Patrol to do, Troy thought without much hope as he followed Peilowski leisurely toward HQ. He shook his head doubtfully. Wilson had told Troy firmly when Troy had begged for a chance to infiltrate that he could not use the Rat Patrol in this situation. Whatever the task, if it was a mission, it would not be against Dietrich. Troy glanced enviously toward the silent ridge. The Jerries had something going up there and Troy wanted to find out what it was.

Wilson was seated at a table at the back of the tent when Troy followed Peilowski inside. Although he was wearing his white varnished helmet, he was concentrating on paperwork. He glanced up, nodded his head at Troy and consulted a code book. Troy watched him with growing curiosity. Wilson was a proper officer schooled at the Point. Whether at base or in the field, he did not wear his helmet at his desk. Something had happened that had stirred him.

"Here, Peilowski," Wilson said, handing him the message form. "Have Locke request immediate confirmation and you wait for it." He looked steadily at Troy without speaking until the first sergeant was away from the tent. Then he asked quietly, "Had enough of your cave in the sand?"

"Right," Troy exclaimed enthusiastically. "You have a mission for us?"

"Good," Wilson said with a fleeting smile. "Yes, I have a little job for the Rat Patrol. I have just sent a message to G2 at Cairo. If my request is confirmed, you will be prepared to depart from this position within four hours."

"Depart?" Troy's spirits sagged. "I'd rather hoped we might be given a shot at Dietrich. Where are we going and what is the mission?"

"For reasons of security, you will be briefed by G2 at your destination."

Troy felt a quick surge of anger. "For reasons of security? I don't understand."

"I'm sorry, Troy," Wilson said and smiled. "It isn't a question of confidence in the Rat Patrol. The risks involved on this assignment are greater than you have ever hazarded. When you arrive at your destination, you will be briefed by G2 on exactly what is required and instructed how to proceed. There is every likelihood that one or all of you will be captured and interrogated. You will know what information you have been told to obtain but not why. The enemy will draw his own conclusions. In such an event the mission will have failed but a vital secret will have been protected. You understand?"

"I don't like to work in the dark," Troy said stubbornly, then suddenly remembering one time when Wilson himself had possessed vital information and had been captured by Dietrich. The Rat Patrol had gone in on orders to rescue him or silence him. He smiled at the recollection. "But I guess I see what you mean. How much can you tell me?"

"Immediately upon confirmation of my request, you will return to your personal quarters." Wilson permitted himself a slight smile at his humor as he consulted his watch. "You will remain there until ten hundred hours at which time you will put on fatigues and steel helmets, leaving your distinctive headgear behind. You will carry canteens and side arms only." He looked sharply at Troy. "Your transportation will be an aircraft. You will need canteens and side arms in the event the plane is shot down. At ten hundred hours, slip away from your rathole." He smiled again at his little joke. "Leave one by one and remain hidden among the supply trucks until the plane has landed. If we're under observation, I don't want the four of you bursting from your camouflage net and racing for the strip when the plane lands. When you board the aircraft, activity to divert attention will be arranged. Is this clear?"

"Loud and clear," Troy said enthusiastically. It was good to have another secret mission to tuck under your web belt.

"I think that covers as much as I can tell you here," Wil-

16

son said, relaxing and looking at Troy with a friendly smile. Abruptly he stood, then walked to the locker at the foot of his cot and opened it. He brought up a bottle of Hennessy Five Star brandy to the table. "Your canteen cup, Troy. We'll have a drink and a cigarette while we wait for Peilowski."

It was not the first time Troy had shared a drink with Wilson but the other occasions had been on the successful completion of a mission, not the start of one. His eyes darted to Wilson and quickly slipped away. The CO had warned of the risks on this assignment, but he seemed very sure of himself, almost smug. Troy remembered that less than half an hour before he had been condemning Wilson for lacking imagination. He puzzled the assignment Wilson could have evolved that made him appear so certain of its success. It must be a very extraordinary job, he concluded.

Peilowski pushed through the opening, red-faced and panting, and thrust a message form at Wilson who scanned his code book, looked at Troy and smiled.

"Confirmed," he said tersely. "You have your instructions."

Troy gulped the last of the warming brandy, replaced his canteen cup, stood and touched his hand to the brim of his hat. He was feeling mellow toward Wilson, and it wasn't from the dollop of brandy.

Wilson nodded and Troy turned to leave. "Peilowski," he heard Wilson say abruptly. "Tell Corporal Locke to be alert for additional information."

Peilowski panted back out of the tent. Troy smiled. A radio operator like Locke didn't have to be told to be alert. He turned to Wilson and waited.

"One final but extremely important warning," Wilson said, stern now. "I perhaps am saying more than I should but I know you men and G2 does not. You will instruct your men that your individual characteristics are well known to the enemy. I want you personally to check out Tully and Hitch. See that Tully has no matchsticks and Hitch has no supply of gum. On this mission, nothing must identify you as the Rat Patrol. To all intents and purposes, for the next few days the Rat Patrol will be very much in evidence in and about this position."

17

Troy could not refrain from asking, "Who and what will we be?"

Wilson hesitated, then smiled quickly, teeth flashing in his tanned face. "I will not say who and what you will be but I will say what you will be doing. You will be assisting Dietrich in capturing the Rat Patrol."

3

Herr Hauptmann Hans Dietrich, commander of a crack Afrika Korps armored unit, stood motionless on top of a flat rock on the gray ridge where his tanks and guns commanded the pass and slope. As he had done each midmorning since he had occupied this well-prepared position guarding the route to Tunis at the western edge of the Cyrenaica peninsula, he observed the Allied camp beyond his reach below. His eyes were thoughtful as he lowered his field glasses. There seemed to be no unusual activity at the Allied position, no indication that the American Colonel Wilson was aware that he was bringing up additional armor at night, a few tanks at a time, and camouflaging them between the remnants of his column. Soon, a week at the most, and his mobile armor would pound down the slope through the safe passage in the minefield and sweep the enemy from the desert floor. He smiled thinly at the thought.

Although his position here on the ridge was secure and blocked the way to western Libya, most of the territory deep on the peninsula he once had commanded had been seized through the treachery of men who had no place in honorable warfare. He bristled at thought of the Rat Patrol. He could not permit the miserable rout of his forces

18

from his former command post at Sidi Abd to remain unavenged. Soon he would start the long trail back.

He searched once more as he did each morning for the four men of the Rat Patrol and their jeeps. He did not fear them. In fact, he was well prepared for the Rat Patrol, should they attempt to penetrate or attack his position, yet he felt reassured each day they and their jeeps still were in the camp. He was prepared to receive them with the fiery reception they had earned, yes, yet he could not entirely anticipate them. Sergeant Troy had a habit of leading his little group in unexpected assaults that usually were costly to the Afrika Korps.

As he watched now, he saw the Rat Patrol crawl from the hollow in the sand where they so foolishly imagined their camouflage nets concealed them from the heights. The four of them in their impertinent headpieces pulled the nets aside and the two drivers backed the jeeps up the sand ramp onto the desert. Sergeant Troy, in his cocky bush hat, leaped into the back of the machine Private Hitchcock was driving and Sergeant Moffitt in his dark beret jumped behind the machine gun in the other. Now they would go racing off side by side in reckless and empty attempts to impress the tank crews with their daring.

But this morning the jeep with Sergeant Troy sped northward toward the sea while the other with Sergeant Moffitt darted south in the direction of the salt marsh. Dietrich scowled. Such an action in broad daylight was clearly for his benefit. It could mean nothing. The jeeps could be observed all of the way to the ocean and to the salt marsh. Yet these were slippery, untrustworthy men. You never could tell what tricks they had in their foolish hats.

The handsome German captain with the cold eyes swung on his heel to the stiff-backed lieutenant who was standing at attention some ten feet back.

"Doeppler," Dietrich said. "I want those jeeps observed meticulously every moment. They must not be lost sight of for a minute. I want to know each place they go, where they stop, what the men do. Understand?"

"Ja, Herr Hauptmann," the lieutenant barked, saluted, whirled and marched away.

The distant drone of an aircraft brought Dietrich's
19

glasses back to the sky above the Allied position. It sounded like the engine of a more powerful plane than the observation cub that buzzed like an annoying but harmless insect now and then far from Dietrich's well-protected flanks. He found a flash of silver to the southeast and shuddered involuntarily as he identified the fast-approaching plane as a B-25 Mitchell medium bomber streaking toward the ridge. Until now the Allies had not attempted to bomb his emplacements but the Mitchell with its 3600-pound bomb load was a deadly threat if it was not driven off. Even as he turned to shout, he knew the bomber and the two jeeps of the Rat Patrol were somehow allied in some secret mission.

"Doeppler," he shouted and found himself standing alone between two 88s. Doeppler never was about when he was needed, he thought waspishly even as he remembered he had just ordered the lieutenant to keep the jeeps under observation. "Kraemer," he called and a gaunt-cheeked man with large eyes jumped down from one of the gun carriers.

"Ja," Kraemer said tonelessly. His voice was as sad as his face.

"Kraemer," Dietrich snapped, irritated at the man's indifference. "Elevate the AA guns, be prepared for a bombing run. That is a Mitchell coming over."

"Ja, mèin Hauptmann," Kraemer said quietly. "The aircraft was observed. The guns are ready. But it is not coming over, I think. Already it has landed on the airstrip of the enemy."

"Dummkopf, why did you not say so?" Dietrich asked angrily, leaping back on the rock.

"Herr Hauptmann?"

"Silence," Dietrich said, bringing his glasses to focus on the bomber. He was just in time to see two men in steel helmets and fatigues clambering aboard the plane. Who were they; what were they; had there been others? he demanded of himself in frustration. During the moments he had been calling for the inept Doeppler and engaged in worthless conversation with the inadequate Kraemer, the bomber had landed. He had no idea what cargo or personnel it had discharged—or what personnel had boarded. Something more important than bombing the ridge was

20

taking place under his nose. It was incredible. Now, would the Mitchell and the men who had boarded, specialists no doubt, rendezvous with one or other jeep of the Rat Patrol? What new bedevilment could he expect from this operation that involved the two jeeps of the Rat Patrol and a medium bomber? Or had the two jeeps of the Rat Patrol traveling in opposite directions been nothing more than a deceptive action to divert his attention from the bomber?

"*Herr Hauptmann,*" Kraemer persisted.

"*Tölpel,* are you stuck here in the ground like a stick?" Dietrich said. "Why aren't you at the gun?"

"I wished only to remind the captain that the Messerschmitts are already overdue for the strafing run that was promised for this morning," Kraemer said calmly. "If they could catch the bomber on the ground——"

"I do not need you to think for me," Dietrich barked, raging at the Rat Patrol. They disrupted even his normal thought processes. "Kloake, Kloake!" he called at the top of his voice for his radio operator as he ran toward the communications truck. "Raise me the fighter planes."

The B-25J bomber had not carried a full crew for its short run to pick up the Rat Patrol. There was a gunner in the turret behind the cockpit and a tail gunner but the .50 caliber guns at each side of the fuselage were not manned. Troy had tumbled into the bare belly of the plane and taken one of the positions so he might observe the country over which they flew through the plexiglass. Moffitt took the position on the other side while Tully and Hitch seemed content to sprawl on the floor. The skin of the ship trembled with a whining vibration as the twin engines snarled and spit and roared. The ship skimmed down the sand runway and lifted with a suddenness that pitched Troy's stomach into his boots. The plane circled to a southeasterly course and Moffitt looked inquiringly across at Troy.

Troy shrugged. He had told the others as much as he knew and could only guess at their destination. He assumed the bomber had come from the base at Bir el Alam. It was now flying in that direction, but that did not mean it would land there. It did not seem likely that an action against Dietrich—or rather, *with* Dietrich, he

21

amended with a grimace—would be mounted from Bir el Alam.

Troy frankly was baffled. Utterly confused and confounded. He had accused the CO of being unimaginative and yet Wilson had concocted some scheme that would enable the four of them to get behind Dietrich's lines and help him capture the Rat Patrol. It not only sounded cockeyed, it was crazy. Even Moffitt, who usually had an answer to a riddle, was puzzled. The only suggestion Troy had been able to offer was that Wilson proposed to parachute them into Dietrich's position in Jerry uniform. That not only would be unimaginative but downright stupid. In the first place, Dietrich knew them all by sight. In the second place, when Dietrich laid his hands on them, he'd have them shot as spies.

The bomber was flying low at about a thousand feet and the growl of the engines rose and fell rhythmically. Below the desert was empty, although it was crisscrossed with the tracks from the supply trucks that shuttled between the base and the Allied position. Watching the monotonous pattern of running lines on the glinting desert floor made Troy drowsy. His eyes were heavy and his head dropped, only to jerk back wide-awake with his hands reaching for the machine gun as the tail-gun hammered. A shadow swooped overhead and the turret gunner behind the cockpit rattled off a burst. A second fighter made a pass at the bomber and the ship shuddered as 20 mm. cannon opened wounds up the spine of its back.

Troy ripped off his helmet and slammed on the earphones.

". . . under attack by two ME-109s," the pilot was saying. "Will attempt evasive action."

Across the fuselage, Moffitt's gun rattled as one of the 109s swept up from below, stabbing at the bomber's belly. Troy's stomach soared into his throat as the ship abruptly dropped until it brushed the desert. Troy brought his gun up and when the 109s made their diving stabs they were met with the fire of four .50 caliber machine guns. The ship shook from the firing, but it was not hit. The big seventeen hundred horsepower engines pulled it up near its top speed of three hundred and twenty miles an hour only feet above the desert and the propellers whipped a furious sand gale.

The ME-109s made one more diving pass at the almost impossible target. When they pulled out of the dives that must have almost pulled their wings off, they shot away to the west. After a few minutes, the bomber climbed back to a thousand feet and throttled back to a comfortable cruising speed.

Troy pushed the earphone forward on his temples as he heard the pilot asking cheerfully, "Was that farewell party for the four of you back there in the belly?"

Troy looked at Moffitt and wrinkled his forehead. Moffitt's eyes were crescents as he shook his head and showed his palms helplessly. On the floor, both Tully and Hitch were looking at Troy inquiringly.

"I don't know," he shouted back above the thunder of the engines.

Less than four hours had passed since Wilson had radioed for the transportation. Dietrich could not possibly have known a bomber was coming to pick up the Rat Patrol. Even in security code, Wilson would not have spelled out who the personnel were that he wanted taken off. Yet he had contacted G2 at Cairo with some plan and he may have felt it necessary to provide details. He'd said they would be briefed at destination by G2 so he must have said something in his message. Troy wondered whether their cover, whatever it was, and their mission, wherever it was, already was known to the enemy.

The aircraft began to rattle through its fuselage as they lost altitude in a fast approach and Troy felt the pressure in his ears. He looked down through the plexiglass and confirmed his suspicions about their destination. They were coming down for a typical hell-down-the-runway landing at Bir el Alam's airbase. The pattern of the buildings at the military installation was familiar, but even better remembered from the days when Wilson's armored column had occupied the town was the jumble of flat-topped, white-walled buildings of the town. There was the oasis, the feathery palms bordering the asphalt road the Allies had built to the base. He even thought he recognized the rooftop cafe where Wilson had entertained the four of them after they'd rescued him from Dietrich at Sidi Abd. They'd had Dietrich himself prisoner for a time on that caper.

Enemy though he was, Troy could almost think of Die-

23

trich as an old friend. Certainly he was an old acquaint-
ance. It seemed that most of their forays had been directed
against the wily Jerry officer. Troy was sure Dietrich held
no such feeling toward the Rat Patrol. As victors, they
could indulge themselves. As the vanquished, Dietrich
must hate their guts.

The bomber touched, settled, raced toward the end of
the runway, reversed props, swung fast and taxied back
beyond the administrative building toward a corrugated
hangar off an asphalt apron at the far end of the field.
Again the props reversed, the tail of the plane swung
around, and the B-25 idled close to the open ended hangar.

"End of the line," the pilot called on the intercom. "Get
under cover fast."

With the bomber blocking view of the hangar, Troy,
followed by Tully, Hitch and Moffitt, dropped to the asphalt and ran into the building. It seemed to be empty. At
the far back corner a partitioned area appeared to provide
a fairly large office. Troy trotted toward it, seeing as he ran
an ancient model open touring car parked at the back of
the hangar. It had tall sides, high fenders and a huge flat-
faced radiator.

"Would you give a look at that!" Hitch exclaimed, pointing at the old car. He broke toward it.

Troy glanced over his shoulder. They were well screened
from view inside the building and he followed Hitch.

"It's sure enough a sweet potato," Tully called, running
ahead with Hitch.

Troy chuckled. It scarcely seemed a thing of beauty to
him with its clumsy, high-riding chassis. He thought he had
seen similar automobiles in old gangster movies. "What is
it?" he asked.

"Hispano-Suiza," Hitch said. "Italian. One of the best in
its day."

"Still is," Tully affirmed.

"How long ago was its day?" Troy asked with a smile.

"This one, probably twenty-six or twenty-seven," Hitch
said.

"But used more recently than that, quite likely," Moffitt
observed. "This probably was Italian staff."

"You think this is a captured Italian staff car?" Troy
asked, interested. "An old buggy like this?"

24

"Some general or other," Moffitt said, nodding. "Possibly old Electric Whiskers himself."

Troy smiled at the reference to the bearded Italian general who had been more successful at running and hiding than at standing and fighting. "It seems to be in good shape."

Hitch and Tully had lifted the hood and were examining the engine.

"Hey," Hitch said. "This baby has been worked over. Some aircraft mechanic has got hold of some real transportation for himself."

"And he plans to make use of it," Troy said, looking into the enormous back seat. Ten five-gallon gasoline cans and two five-gallon water cans were lined in three rows on the floor. He stepped onto the running board and lifted one. It was full.

The car had been a seven-passenger job, but the jump seats had been removed. The red leather upholstery had seen some rough usage but the tears had been mended. The instrument panel was clean and the large steering wheel had been spliced where it had been broken. The windshield was high and straight. Keys were in the ignition switch, Troy noticed as Tully opened the door on the driver's side and slid behind the steering wheel.

"I sure would like to give this one a whirl," Tully said enviously, working the wheel forth and back.

"Well, why don't you start it?" a voice broke in behind and Troy swung about.

A man with a high forehead; pleasant, tanned face and crinkled brown eyes had quietly approached them, apparently from the partitioned area. He was bareheaded, his thin brown hair revealing a sunburned scalp. He was smoking a pipe and wore a short-sleeved khaki shirt without insignia and suntan trousers. He was smiling.

He indicated each in turn as he spoke his name: "Troy, Moffitt, Tully, Hitch. I'm Norman, G2."

Troy wondered what his rank was, not that it made any difference.

"Go ahead, Tully, start it, drive it around the hangar." You might as well get acquainted with it. That car is going to take you behind the Jerry lines."

25

4

When Norman had told them the old Hispano-Suiza was going to take them behind the Jerry lines, Troy's immediate thought was that they were going in as Italian officers. He had been almost right in one respect and very wrong in another, he thought now, six hours later. He examined himself again in the full-length mirror and shook his head. He still couldn't believe what he saw.

Like the others, he was wearing civilian clothing. His suit was double-breasted with padded shoulders. The material was flannel, moss green with yellow stripes. His silk apple-green shirt was also striped with yellow and his wide tie was splashed with yellow flowers. His pants were pegged and his shoes were pointed. As should have been his head, he thought with a grin.

He turned to Moffitt, whose cream-colored gabardine suit was single-breasted with a pinched waist. Moffitt's eyes became crescents as he nodded his head at Tully and Hitch. Tully sported a double-breasted tobacco-brown gabardine with which he wore a dark brown silk shirt and a bright yellow tie. Hitch's single-breasted suit was purple and his shirt was pink.

"Come now," Moffitt said with a throaty chuckle. "You can't really mean this is the way you chaps dress in America."

"Not if we can help it," Troy said wryly, looking at the sparkle of the synthetic two-carat diamond on his left pinkie.

But it was not the clothing that had made the big transformation. Troy examined himself again in the mirror. His hair was black, curly and tousled, and grew low on the nape of his neck. His sideburns were lengthy and he supported an abundant mustache. It was his eyes that startled him the most. They had changed in color from tawny to brown. Hitch's and Tully's matched Troy's while Moffitt's were somewhat darker. Moffitt, Hitch and Tully also wore unruly caps of curly black hair. And like Troy, each of the others sprouted black bristles on his upper lip.

The Rat Patrol had been transmogrified. They now were the Enna brothers from Enna, high in the heartland mountains of Sicily, but late of Chicago, U.S.A.

"The deception is bold enough to succeed," Norman had said softly with a slow smile when he'd taken them into the hangar office after Tully had driven the Hispano-Suiza around the building and pronounced it sound.

The office itself was a deception, Troy had thought in disbelief, wondering how so much had been accomplished in so short a time. It was a theatrical dressing room. A table with three lighted mirrors held assorted jars and boxes. Next to it was a full-length mirror. A straight chair stood under a powerful light in the middle of the room. Two trunks were open, displaying prop material, and four violin cases leaned against a wall. Two Army cots had been pushed against another wall and a hawk-nosed man in a white jacket sat on one of them. He stood, fixing each in turn with piercing brown eyes.

"Bernard, G2," Norman introduced him succinctly.

Bernard nodded curtly.

"Time is short," Norman said. "You should leave as soon as it is dark, which gives us about six hours. I'll brief you as the doctor works. Troy, if you'll remove your helmet and fatigues. Take a seat in the straight chair under the light."

What crazy kind of caper is this, Troy asked himself as Doctor Bernard threw a barber's apron around Troy's neck. Bernard switched on electric shears and ran the clippers up Troy's sideburns. Hitch, Tully and even Moffitt were staring at him speechlessly.

"First, your mission," Norman said quietly. "You are to obtain precise locations of the enemy's armor, emplacements, machine gun and mortar installations, and infantry positions at the ridge where Wilson is stalled. You also are to obtain the pattern of the minefield and chart the safe passageway."

Troy whistled softly as the clippers whirred and his hair fell onto the barber's towel. If they were successful in getting behind Dietrich's lines, it would not be difficult to obtain weapons locations, but the pattern of the minefield was something else. So Wilson had had a brainstorm after all. Troy glanced at the violin cases. He shook his head. Dietrich wasn't going to go for a stringed quartet on the firing line.

"Your approach to Dietrich will be from the direction of Tunis in the Hispano-Suiza," Norman continued. "You are black marketeers, former U.S. hoodlums who fled through Mexico and have taken refuge in Sicily. Forged passports and documents have been prepared. The forgeries are obvious. With your backgrounds, Dietrich would be suspicious if you had genuine papers. You now are operating in the black market between Spain and ports of convenience in Africa. If Dietrich checks your story, it will be confirmed in Tunis through our agent whose cover is the black market. You will approach Dietrich because you have something to sell him."

Bernard whipped off the towel from Troy's neck and shook off the hair. Tully guffawed at Troy's bare head. Hitch glumly watched the operation.

"We don't speak Italian," Troy warned.

"You are American gangsters with Sicilian antecedents," Norman said calmly.

"Moffitt's accent will give him away," Troy said as Bernard fitted a wig over his pate, stepped back, eyed it critically, shook his head and dug into the trunk for another.

"Button your lip, punk," Moffitt snarled with a sneer which quickly became a smile that lighted his eyes. "I've done a bit of acting, you know. This should be a jolly good time."

Bernard had found a wig that suited him and now he was affixing it to Troy's scalp with a liquid adhesive. "This will itch," he said, "but it can't be helped. You can scratch when it itches. It won't come off."

"What do we have to sell Dietrich?" Troy asked as Bernard lathered his face and started to shave him. He was

28

beginning to enjoy the idea of this mission almost as much as Moffitt apparently did. Hitch was scowling.

"Among other things, you are experienced gunmen," he said. Troy glanced at the violin cases and laughed aloud. Norman nodded and smiled. "Yes, the European idea of an American gangster is Thirty-ish. The tommy guns in the violin cases will be clinchers. This is what you have to sell Dietrich: he has tried to capture or destroy the Rat Patrol and failed. You know this because it is common knowledge among the German military in Tunis. It is more than knowledge—it is a standing joke. Lay it on as thick as you like. It will enrage him. For a fee, you will find them, gun them down or kidnap them. Nab, I believe the word is. This should put you on speaking terms with Dietrich. Now you're in the enemy's camp. You know what is required. From this point on, you're on your own, although we'll give you what assistance we can. In two days, the jeeps and the men who are impersonating you will disappear to put Dietrich in a receptive mood."

Bernard had fixed a mustache on Troy's lip. "One thing, Sergeant," he said crisply, turning to the others. "This goes for all of you. You must shave every day, twice if necessary. Do not let the stubble of your own beards betray you."

Troy stepped to the dressing table and looked at himself in the mirror. He looked at a stranger. "The eyes don't look right," he said.

"We'll fit you and the others with colored contact lenses after I've finished barbering," Bernard said and smiled for the first time. "Don't worry. I am an opthamologist in civilian life. The lenses will give you no difficulty. They are held in place by surface tension of the eye fluid."

Moffitt took the chair next and then Tully. Although the transformations were taking place before his eyes, Troy could not believe these were the men he had known.

"We could pad the cheeks, build up the noses, perform other small tricks," Bernard said as he finished with Tully. "Usually it is not necessary. Hair, eyes and clothes ordinarily do the trick." He beckoned to Hitch.

"You're not going to cut my hair," Hitch said sulkily.

Norman laughed and said, "A red-haired Sicilian is a rare bird indeed."

29

"I'm a rare bird then," Hitch said stubbornly. "You aren't going to cut it."

"We don't have time," Bernard began impatiently.

"It's all right, Doctor," Troy said easily. "Don't cut his hair. The three of us can handle this. He doesn't have to come along."

From the corners of his eyes, Troy saw a smile playing on Moffitt's lips. Hitch glowered and got into the chair without a word. He sat sullen and silent all the time the clippers scattered his hair about his shoulders and into his lap.

"We'll fit these and then I'm going to give you something special, Sergeant," Bernard said after he helped Troy put the lenses on. To Troy's surprise he was not conscious of them and they did not seem to change his vision. "Open your mouth, please."

Bernard examined Troy's front teeth, opened a small leather case and fiddled in it. With a tweezers, he picked up a small piece of gold leaf, fitted the foil around a left incisor, took out the cap he'd made and painted the tooth with a liquid. He slipped the gold cap over the tooth, adjusted and trimmed the gold.

"It is a special cement not affected by moisture," Bernard said. "We will remove the cap with solvent when the masquerade is over." He smiled. "Unless you decide to keep it."

Now Troy flashed a gold-toothed smile at himself in the mirror, turned to the pile of hats on the table. He selected a snap-brimmed grey felt and set it square on his head the way he wore his bush hat.

"I advise against the hats," Bernard said. "They ruin the effect of the hair."

"We need protection against the sun," Troy said.

"Your wigs afford that," Bernard said. "Your scalps are insulated."

Troy shrugged and slouched over to Hitch and Tully. A cigarette dangled indolently from a corner of Tully's mouth. "You guys ready?" Troy growled.

"Let's scram," Tully said with curled lip and narrowed eyes.

Moffitt chuckled and Hitch cracked the glum face he'd

worn ever since he'd lost his hair. He laughed aloud.

"You're a ham, Tully," Moffitt said.

"Southern style," Tully conceded.

The four of them went to the wall and each picked up a violin case. The tommy guns had been checked out during the alteration sessions.

"Your bags are already in the car," Norman said, holding them a moment. "You'll find shaving equipment, changes of clothing, other items appropriate to your new status. With the exception of Tully, your own first names have been used on the passports and papers. Sam, Jack, Mark—they're common enough—but Tully's is made out to Sol Enna. Practice using it on the trip."

The Enna brothers filed out of the office. Through the open end of the hangar, Troy could see the marker lights along the runway glowing in the dark of early evening. The yellow headlights of a noisy tractor ran across the apron. Lights from the administration building reached out to touch the runway and a B-25 hulked in shadow on the other side. Norman and Bernard followed them to the Hispano-Suiza. Tully slid behind the wheel, Hitch beside him in the front seat, and Troy and Moffitt climbed into the rear that still allowed them room to stretch their legs even with the cans and baggage. Tully turned the switch and started the whispering motor.

"Good luck, men," Norman called and Bernard waved.

"Can it, mugs," Troy rasped at Norman and Bernard. The G2 men were A-1 in his book, but he hoped they were at least majors.

Bernard chuckled and Norman was laughing as he walked rapidly to the office. Tully wheeled the big touring car without lights to the end of the hangar, braked and waited with the motor idling silently. The wail of a siren shivered on the desert air and the lights all over Bir el Alam blinked out. Tully eased the car from the hangar, across the apron and onto the runway. It was a cooling, moonless night, but the sky was iridescent and Troy could plainly see the skeleton outline of the tower, the buildings and the B-25. Tully drove west the length of the runway, turned south along the link fence and followed it to a gate which swung open as they approached. Troy heard the gate screech and clack as it closed after them. Tully turned right onto a graded road and picked up speed as they left the base behind.

"This security seems foolish after we were jumped by the 109s," Troy said to Moffitt. Even without a moon he could make out Moffitt's features.

"Coincidence," Moffitt said calmly. "I don't think Jerry had the faintest we were aboard. Those two birds have buzzed us regularly. Today the bomber was there, so why not take a swipe at it? Moreover, old boy, if you thought we'd been uncovered, why didn't you mention it to Norman?"

"And take a chance of losing out on this caper?" Troy demanded with a tight smile.

"It is a fantastic mission," Moffitt agreed and his teeth showed whitely. "Shall we open a bag and see what we're carrying?"

"Norman said toilet articles, changes of clothing," Troy said indifferently.

"He also said articles appropriate to hoodlums," Moffitt reminded him. "I'm curious what is considered appropriate to our new stations in life."

"Go ahead, then," Troy said. "Open your own. They're tagged."

Despite his indifference, Troy watched closely as Moffitt lifted two bags, checking the tags in the flame of the gold-plated lighter which matched the gold-plated cigarette case he had been issued. Troy had paid little attention to the bags, but now he saw they were the European type travel bag with zip tops and two side pockets. The leather was soft—buffalo, he thought—expensive but worn. Moffitt found the bag that was tagged J. Enna and opened the outside pockets first. One contained a carton of cigarettes, the other a long, slim silver flask. Moffitt unscrewed the flask and sniffed.

"Bourbon," he said. He sounded disappointed and handed the flask to Troy.

"I'll get my own," Troy said, interested now. He lighted his silver cigarette lighter and the synthetic diamond on his little finger glimmered. "Hitch," he called as he lifted the first bag. "Whoa—Mark," he corrected himself, handing the bag over the cans across the wide back seat. "Sol."

32

Hitch took Tully's bag. Troy felt the outline of the cigarette carton and removed the flask from the other pocket. He tasted the bourbon. It was smooth, bonded stuff. He drank again and replaced the flask. Inside his fingers felt the slippery touch of silk.

"Silk shirts, silk shorts," he groaned.

"I believe mine are linen, no cambric," Moffitt said and Troy knew he was smiling.

"I've got a wool sweater with a turtle neck," Hitch called back.

"They didn't make the mistake of duplicating," Troy said, relieved. "I'll bet none of the things are new."

"Did you know there's booze in the flask?" Hitch asked.

"Sure," Troy said with a smile. "I know, but how did you find out?"

Troy explored below the silk, found a leather toilet kit and then his hand touched steel. He brought out a snub-nosed Browning automatic. His fingers ran along the side of the bag until they found a box of cartridges. He ejected the magazine from the pistol, loaded it, replaced the cartridge box in the bag and shoved the gun in his coat pocket. It was an authentic touch and it might come in handy.

"Tully—I mean, Sol—has a fancy frog sticker in his bag," Hitch said. "I didn't get a weapon."

"You've got your gat," Troy reminded him. "You can always pick up a piece of rope for a garrote."

"They seem to be well acquainted with us for such short notice," Moffitt observed.

"Yes, don't they?" Troy said dryly as he found a bottle of bourbon at the bottom of his bag. His hand grasped a bundle of paper that had the greasy feel of money. He removed it and his lighter showed him a bundle of twenty-dollar bills.

"You get any of these?" he asked, showing the money to Moffitt.

"Only what is in the wallet they issued," Moffitt said. "About two hundred dollars. It should suffice."

Troy counted the bills. There were a hundred of them. Bribe money. He put them back in the bag and zipped it shut.

They had driven by the last building and the graded road deteriorated into a track that ran northwest. This was the old trade route they would follow for almost a hundred miles before lurching off through the unmarked sand and rock south of the salt marsh. Troy heard the moan of the all-clear signal and turned as the lights of Bir el Alam twinkled on again.

"Okay for me to use lights, Sam?" Tully asked over his shoulder.

"Ohh!" Troy groaned with a fleeting smile. "I can see what this caper is going to cost me. Sure, it should be safe to use them for the next couple hours. Have to, if we're going to make any time."

The big headlights poked holes in the night. Tully switched on the long-reaching searchlight mounted at the side of the windshield, adjusted it and turned off the headlights. Someplace ahead in the night a rifle cracked. The second shot made a spiderwebbed hole in the windshield directly between Tully and Hitch.

5

Shrieking protests that rose and fell in an incoherent babble brought Wilson from his table where he was digging his supper of rubbery cheese from a ration can. He stepped quickly from the acetylene lamp light in the tent into the alley behind the halftracks where the reddish light from small fires made the night seem darker. He could hear the sounds of struggling and grunts above the cries in Arabic. The commotion was coming from behind HQ and he stepped to the side of the tent, looking toward the supply trucks. As his eyes adjusted to the gloom, he saw a man wearing an Australian bush hat and another wearing a French Foreign Legion cap plodding toward him. Between them they dragged a screaming, kicking, robed figure. He stepped back beyond the light that crept onto the sand through the open flap of his tent.

"What's this?" he asked sharply as the bluish light fell on the trio.

"Thief," said the man in the bush hat.

"Or spy," said the man in the Foreign Legion cap.

"Two other Ay-rabs got away," the man in the bush hat said.

"Take him into HQ," Wilson said irritably. The Arabs were more of an annoyance than sand fleas. You never knew whether they came to steal or spy for the enemy. "I'll get the Eskimo."

Kalmuk, the Eskimo, was Corporal Locke's assistant, the second radio operator. The flat-faced Eskimo who'd found his ways through the mysterious channels of the Army was a linguist who spoke not only German and French but who had mastered half a dozen Arabic dialects as well.

"Sure, boss," Kalmuk said easily, turning his bright black eyes from the Command Set to Wilson. "Johnny was bringing me a cup of coffee anyway. He can take over and I'll be in right away."

When Wilson returned to his tent, the Arab was trussed hand and foot, yelling obscenely and writhing on the sand.

"We can't have this," he said angrily. "Untie the ropes."

"He was biting and scratching," the man in the bush hat said. He was a chunky slab of beef, built like a wrestler with no neck. His eyes were small and his lips were thin.

"You're Corporal Merriam," Wilson said with a frown, and then glanced at the man in the Foreign Legion cap. He was brawny and his jaw was square. "And you're Corporal Heath. Transportation. Correct?"

"We're truck drivers," Merriam mumbled.

"Before that you were MPs," Wilson said harshly. "That's why you were selected for this job. You know how to restrain a man. Untie the ropes."

"That Ay-rab stinks," Merriam blurted.

"Heath, remove the ropes," Wilson ordered. "Merriam, restrain the prisoner. Now tell me what happened."

Merriam grasped the Arab by one wrist, and as Heath cut the ropes that bound his arms, Merriam brought the wrist up sharply behind the prisoner's back. The Arab screeched in pain. When Heath cut the bonds about his feet, he kicked Heath savagely in the stomach. Heath grunted. Merriam jerked the pinioned arm, twisting at the same time, and the Arab yelped shrilly.

"On your feet, your garbage-eating pig," Merriam snarled, viciously yanking the Arab by his arm.

The Arab uttered a sobbing moan.

"That's enough, Merriam," Wilson snapped. He studied the prisoner. The Arab was a miserable specimen. He had beady, ferret-like eyes that seemed to burn red at the edges of the black pupils. He did not look like a man of the desert. His face was saffron and pocked. Filthy, ragged robes draped his thin shoulders and he did not stand tall. Merriam had been right: the foul odor of the man contaminated the tent.

Heath was rubbing his stomach were the Arab had kicked him, but suddenly the grimace on his face changed to a grin. "We caught him in a net, like a fish," he said.

The prisoner started to struggle and Merriam gritted his teeth, exerting slow, steady pressure to his arm until the man bent back in agony. "Once more," Merriam grated, "and I'll break it off."

"Once more, Corporal, and I'll break *you*," Wilson said in a hard, flat voice. "I said restrain, not torture. Now tell me what happened."

Merriam's little eyes were resentful. "We crawled out of that cave for some air." His voice was surly. "We took a walk to the landing strip. We come back through the trucks. There was these three Ay-rabs pawing in one of them. We grabbed at them. They ran. The other two got away. This one ran smack into the net over the jeeps. We nailed him."

Probably no more than another petty Arab thief, Wilson thought. Jerry had no need to send spies into the camp. It was open, everything could be observed from the ridge. Unless, he abruptly realized, Dietrich's suspicions had been aroused by the bomber that did not bomb, by the four men who had boarded the aircraft. His eyes narrowed thoughtfully. Perhaps it was a good thing this man had been taken by Merriam and Heath in their unorthodox headgear. He would question the prisoner briefly and release him.

The Eskimo stepped briskly into the tent, went directly to the table, about-faced and studied the Arab. Kalmuk's black eyes were troubled and his broad nose seemed to be pinched in distaste when he turned to Wilson.

"This is no desert Arab," he said. "He is a rat that has crawled from under a wharf."

"Then it is fitting he should have been captured by the Rat Patrol," Wilson said. The man probably didn't understand English, but it was worth a try. Kalmuk's eyelids flickered but he remained silent. "Ask him what he was doing here, in French and German."

The Arab's beady eyes showed no comprehension when Kalmuk spoke to him.

"All right," Wilson said wearily. "Arabic."

This time Kalmuk spoke sharply. The Arab spat at him. Merriam gave his arm a wicked upward thrust. The Arab cried in agony. Kalmuk repeated the question. The prisoner threw a torrent of bitter words at him.

"He says it is his country," Kalmuk said, turning to Wilson. "He says *we* should answer that question."

"And the Italians and the Germans," Wilson said under his breath. "Ask him what he was doing in this camp."

Kalmuk spoke to the prisoner and Merriam emphasized the importance of the question by wrenching the arm again. The Arab jabbered.

"He says he was hungry and looking for something to eat," Kalmuk said.

"In the trucks?" Wilson commented dryly. "Where did he come from? How did he get here? Where is he going?"

The Arab told Kalmuk that he was from the tribe of el Burabub near Siwa.

"He is lying," Kalmuk said. "Siwa is an oasis near the Qattara Depression in Egypt. He could never have come so far on foot. Also, Siwa is the English word for the place. The Arabs have another word for it. It isn't much use to question him. He will say what he pleases and it will be nothing but a pack of lies."

"You're right, Kalmuk," Wilson said.

"What're we going to do? Hold him?" Merriam asked.

"What good would it do?" Wilson asked. "His two companions got away. Turn him loose. There's nothing he can tell. March him out of camp. Kalmuk, tell him the next Arab we find in camp will be shot on sight. We'll double the guard."

Wilson watched Merriam propel the dirty Arab out of the tent, and decided that the man who was impersonating Troy, like many MPs, had a sadistic streak in him. Wilson did not approve of cruelty and hoped the man did not suffer any further rough treatment. It could be difficult for the Rat Patrol if the Arab was a spy for the Jerries and reported to Dietrich that the men in the strange hats had captured him and mistreated him. From afar, Wilson thought he heard a sharp cry of pain but it might have been a jackal.

The three Arabs walked into Dietrich's lines with Schmeisser machine pistols in their backs. Behind the three members of the patrol that had captured them, a corporal led the fine tawny horses they had been riding. Herr Hauptmann Hans Dietrich was seated in a canvas camp chair enjoying a brandy after a reasonably palatable supper of roast kid, when Doeppler informed him of the captives.

"Arabs!" Dietrich exclaimed. "On the ridge? But it is impossible."

"*Ja, Herr Hauptmann,* that is so," Doeppler agreed stiffly. His lantern jaw did not seem to move when he spoke. "It is impossible, but here they are."

"Bring them in," Dietrich said frigidly. "We shall find out how this is possible."

The three Arabs were prodded into the tent before him and the three enlisted men from the patrol kept their Schmeissers in their backs. Dietrich's cold eyes appraised them. The man in the middle was tall, erect and proud. He had a typical Arabian hawklike nose and the steady eyes of a falcon. His burnoose and robes were dusty but not dirty. The men on either side were scrawny and filthy, but their dark eyes were defiant. Dietrich noticed that the left arm of the man on the right had been injured. He clutched his robe near the shoulder as if for support.

"Can any one of you speak to me in my language?" he asked hopelessly. No one in his command spoke Arabic.

"We all speak your tongue, *Effendi,*" the tall man in the middle said. He had a jagged scar running diagonally from

38

his right temple across his cheek to the corner of his mouth. The scar appeared to whiten when he spoke.

"What are you doing here on the ridge?" Dietrich demanded. "Do you not know this is a battlefield? The slope is filled up with explosives. You might have been blown in many pieces. How did you get here?"

"We are aware you have mined the approach," the scarred Arab said calmly. "There is a trail through the rocks to this ridge."

"Doeppler!" Dietrich shouted, although the lieutenant was still within the tent not ten feet away. "Take a patrol and one of these Arabs. Have him show you the trail. Mine it from the bottom up. At once."

"*Ja, Herr Hauptmann*," Doeppler said. He turned to the Arab with the injured arm. "Come with me."

"Take the other man, Lieutenant," the tall Arab said. It was an order, not a suggestion, and Dietrich looked at him with some respect. "The man with the broken arm is the one who can tell the most about the American camp."

"What's that?" Dietrich asked.

"There was no need to take us prisoner, Captain," the one who seemed to be the leader said. "We were on our way to you. We have just come from the American camp. We thought you would be interested in what we have seen."

"Yes," Dietrich said cautiously. "Yes, I admit I would be interested in learning what you observed. A moment. Grosse!" he called for his orderly-driver. Grosse stepped into the tent immediately and Dietrich looked at the tall, fair young man appreciatively. Grosse was respectful but not obsequious. "Grosse, chairs for our guests. Coffee also."

"*Ja, mein Hauptmann*," Grosse said.

"Who are you?" Dietrich addressed himself to the tall Arab. "You have worked with us before?"

"I am el Burabub," he said. "My tribe is a ride of a day to the south. The man is Haffi. He is of my tribe but for many years has been at Surt on the sea. We have provided information at one time or another to that one of you they call the Fox."

"You have furnished the Fox with information?" Dietrich said in some surprise. He wondered whether they

39

actually meant Rommel and how far he would have to bargain. "That is good."

"It is understood we are paid for our knowledge," el Burabub said.

"According to its value," Dietrich countered.

"It should be to the satisfaction of he who bears the word," el Burabub said. "Today's bargain is tomorrow's sorrow."

"That also is understood," Dietrich said with a grimace. "How do I know the Americans have not sent you with false information?"

The man called Haffi burst out with a stream of invective in Arabic. "They took me prisoner! They mistreated me!" he said in German.

"If they took you prisoner, why did they let you go?" Dietrich asked coldly.

"They did not know what to do with me," Haffi said. "They said I would not tell them the truth in any case. They told me to warn my tribesmen that every Arab would be shot on sight."

"Oh?" Dietrich said suspiciously. If this was true, Wilson was depriving himself of a valuable source of information. Usually, the Arabs would sell out to the highest bidder.

"We do not know what information will be of value to you," el Burabub said. "From your position here on the ridge you can observe their camp so you know what most of their weapons are, but you have not been in the camp. I think we have discovered something you do not know, but it will be better if you question us first and we will answer if we can. Does this sound like deception to you?"

"No, I believe you," Dietrich said warily.

Grosse came in with two folding chairs. The Arabs seated themselves and in a moment Grosse returned with two tin cups filled with black coffee.

"This is entirely different from the treatment I was given by the Americans," Haffi said.

"How were you treated by the enemy?" Dietrich asked Haffi curiously.

"I was seized and beaten," Haffi said vengefully. "I was tied hands behind and about my feet with rope and thrown upon the sand. When I would not answer their questions,

40

they tortured me. When I was thrown from their camp, my arm was treated so savagely I fear I shall not be able to use it again."

"I think it is broken," el Burabub said simply.

"Who did this to you?" Dietrich asked angrily. "But of course, you would not know."

"I do not think they were of the American military," Haffi said. "One wore the kind of cap the French wore when they were on the desert and the other, the one who was like a beast and maimed my arm, wore a strange hat almost like a civilian."

"The Rat Patrol!" Dietrich said, profoundly shocked.

"The very words they used," Haffi agreed. "They said I was a rat and it was fitting I should be captured by the Rat Patrol."

"But this is savage," Dietrich said in disgust. It confirmed the idea that had been growing in him during the past months. The Rat Patrol were not honorable soldiers. "How was it they caught you?"

"I fell into a pit covered with a net," Haffi said.

The camouflage net that concealed the jeeps, Dietrich thought. He decided he could trust these Arabs and nodded approvingly. Doeppler stepped back into the tent.

"Well?" Dietrich said shortly.

"The way is sealed," Doeppler said.

"There was such a trail leading into this camp?" Dietrich asked.

"*Ja*," Doeppler said.

"This should have been discovered when the first patrol went out," Dietrich said severely. "I shall deal with you later. That is all, Doeppler."

"*Ja, Herr Hauptmann*," Doeppler said sharply. He saluted, about-faced and marched from the tent.

Dietrich turned to el Burabub. "Tell me from the beginning. How was it you happened to be in their camp. Did you go there to steal?"

"Of course," el Burabub said. He seemed surprised at the question. "At the same time, also to observe. We felt certain we would find things of interest to you."

"What things did you find that you think might interest me?" Dietrich asked.

"I hope you will treat us fairly because I do not see how

41

you could otherwise have this information," el Burabub said. "You will know I speak the truth because I do not know what this weapon is that I shall describe to you. Under the net in the pit where Haffi fell, there is concealed a gun with a long thick barrel. It has a shield and is mounted on wheels. It is pointing toward you. In the trucks are many shells that are quite heavy, perhaps thirty kilos or more."

Dietrich gasped. That could mean only that Wilson somehow or other had obtained one of the British twenty-five-pound howitzers, the 87.6 mm. artillery piece that could belt out four rounds a minute of high explosive or armor piercing ammunition. Dietrich felt sick. The gun was effective at a range of twelve thousand five hundred yards.

The Rat Patrol and the jeeps were camouflage, he thought. The bomber today, the strange personnel, the calm in the camp—it could mean only that Wilson was preparing to sit back out of range, shell the hill and ridge from bottom to top with the howitzer and assault the position with his armor when he was satisfied the way was clear. Dietrich chewed his lower lip.

"You are not pleased we brought you this information?" el Burabub asked.

"No, I am not pleased!" Dietrich erupted, immediately apologizing. "It is the information that displeases me. I am very grateful to you, my friend, for bringing it to me."

Dietrich walked slowly to the locker at the foot of his cot. He unlocked it, lifted a heavy strongbox from the locker, opened it and reached in for two handsful of silver florins. He dumped them in el Burabub's lap.

"It is a great deal of money," he said, "but I am willing to pay for something of value. You will return when you have something else of interest."

"We shall return," el Burabub said gravely. He stood and with Haffi, joined the third Arab, who was then standing at the entrance. The corporal brought up the horses and the Arabs rode away to the west. Once, just before they reached the perimeter, Dietrich would have sworn he heard them laughing, but of course, he was wrong. Arabs never laughed.

42

6

You couldn't say it was a typical Rat Patrol maneuver, Troy thought with fleeting grim humor as he tumbled with his violin case from one side of the slewing Hispano-Suiza. Almost with the impact of the rifle slug on the windshield, Tully had switched off the searchlight, jerked the car off the road and spun, it about. Moffitt went out the other side of the back seat as Hitch dived from the front. Tully raced back toward Bir el Alam, now switching on his headlights. A few hundred yards up the trace, the car seemed to falter.

Moffitt and Hitch crouched some ten yards apart on one side of the track and just above them on the other side, Troy had his tommy gun off safety. He was squatting beside a clump of spiney cactus. In a moment he heard the pounding thud of galloping hooves and five robed figures rode into shadowy view in the transparent night. Ahead of the other four, a single horseman guided his mount with his knees as he raised a rifle to his shoulder. Behind, the other four men rode in pairs.

Troy leaped to his feet as the first pair rushed by in a sandy cloud of dust. He fired three bursts point-blank at the second pair of horsemen. Both tumbled from their rearing horses as Troy heard the rattle of several machine gun bursts from the other side of the road. A horse ran wildly back along the trace. A body was dragging from a stirrup and the animal was frenzied. It shook its head violently, rearing and pawing. Troy lifted his gun to shoot it, shook his head. He did not think the animal was wounded and it would free itself from its burden soon. The animal kicked

43

with its hind legs and jerked off the road. The body dropped to the sand and rolled. The horse pranced into the desert. Two other horses already had trotted away.

Troy walked to the first figure lying on the track, jerked back the burnoose, flicked his lighter and knelt holding the flame to the face. The mouth and eyes of a very dead Arab were open. The other man he'd killed also was an Arab. He brushed the sand from his recently acquired suit, went back to the cactus and picked up his violin case. The car had turned around and the glare of its headlights plucked Moffitt and Hitch from the night. As Troy had done, they were bending over their victims inspecting their faces.

Troy stopped in shock. For a moment there was something terribly unreal about the scene. Ahead of him were two sinister strangers, tommy guns dangling, dressed in garish civilian clothing, checking the men they'd just murdered. The Arabs had tried to ambush them and they'd turned the trick, but somehow killing seemed different than when you were in uniform. The sickening moment passed and Troy walked on.

"Arabs?" he asked.

"Yeah," Hitch said, standing. He looked about, stepped off the road and recovered his violin case.

"What do you make of it, Sam?" Moffitt asked quietly, replacing his tommy gun in the case.

The Hispano-Suiza rolled to a stop a few yards away and Tully jumped out, leaving the motor quietly idling.

"A neat maneuver, Sol," he said to Tully, but he was thinking about Moffitt's question. The attempted ambush made him more uneasy than being jumped by the 109s. The two attempts seemed too much for coincidence, but how could anyone have known they'd be driving the old touring car this way just after nightfall? Unless, he thought savagely, Wilson had chattered like a gossipy old biddy when he'd sent the radio message.

"This wagon ain't no jeep, Sam," Tully drawled, "but it's got spunk."

Troy turned to Moffitt. "There's nothing to make of it, Jack," he said. "The Arabs saw a civilian car by itself away from town and thought they had easy pickings."

"Away from town!" Moffitt exclaimed. "Why, we are within sound of the base."

44

"That's right, Jack," Troy said quickly. "We'd better carry the mail."

He ran ahead to remove the bodies from the trace while Moffitt and Hitch bent to their tasks. He had just dragged his second victim into the desert when the car moved up. He stepped onto the running board and swung in beside Moffitt.

"Douse the lamps, Sol," he said from the corner of his mouth. "And open her up. We got to take it on the lam. The fuzz is on our tail."

"What!" Moffitt exclaimed as the headlights went out and the car shot ahead.

"Back there, Jack," Troy said, turning and looking over the tonneau with him. Racing out from the base were two sets of headlights. "You were right. They heard the firing."

Troy and Moffitt settled back as Tully guided the car around a curve, up and over a hill and the lights of Bir el Alam and the MPs, or whoever they were, disappeared.

"Is that the true cant of the criminal?" Moffitt asked curiously.

"If you mean, is that the lingo of the mobster," Troy said with a quick smile, "I don't know. It's the way they talk on radio and in the movies. Ask Sol. He used to run 'shine in the Kentucky ridge country."

"Sam there, he sho nuff rat," Tully half turned and said. "All us gangstahs tawk like thet."

Hitch squirmed about. "You think they'll come after us, Sam? When they find the bodies?"

"No," Troy said shortly. "Why should they complicate their lives over a bunch of Arabs? They'll bury them and forget it."

The big old car had been built for cobblestone pavements and potholed country roads. It did not object to the desert trace. The huge wheels dug into the sand and the Hispano-Suiza rushed through the bluish night with a smooth surge of power. With its high clearance, it would be a better vehicle than the jeeps when they came to the rocky hill country.

Troy considered the route they were taking. For about a hundred miles, they would follow the old trace through the desert. In about two hours they would run out of desert, turning due west off the trail and entering a rough barren

45

land of stony ridges at the western edge of the peninsula. There were salt marshes, three of them, great impenetrable areas, glittering white sloughs that were worse than quicksand. They would snake between on a strip of jagged high land well south of Dietrich's position. Turning northwest beyond the marshes, they should be able to pick up the coastal highway this side of Surt and by the time a Jerry patrol halted them, appear to be approaching from the direction of Tunis far to the northwest. Although it was a trip of not much more than three hundred miles, Troy estimated it would take up to twenty hours, sixteen if they were lucky, twenty-four if they ran into difficulties. For the first hundred miles on the trace, they should be able to maintain a speed of fifty miles per hour. Once they entered the trackless, menacing highland, they would be pressed to make five or ten miles an hour. One third of their journey would be through this inhospitable, empty land between the salt marshes. The final leg of the trip should be reasonably fast. It would be better, Troy thought, if they were presented to Dietrich at dusk the next afternoon when the fading light would contribute to their disguises.

Moffitt had been fumbling with a flap on the side of the door. He lifted it and reached into the pocket. "I wondered whether they hadn't provided us with a few pineapples," he said with a chuckle. He brought out a Jerry stick grenade and showed it to Troy.

"That's a potato masher, not a pineapple," Troy observed. He turned to the pocket in his door. "How many are there?"

He found the pocket on his side was stuffed with the German grenades and started to count them.

"A dozen," Moffitt said.

"Another dozen here," Troy said. He was pleased at their find. A grenade was a somewhat more positive weapon of both offense and defense than a tommy gun. "I wonder why Norman didn't mention them."

"I imagine they assumed we'd have intelligence enough to realize that since we are the Enna brothers, we are equipped appropriately," Moffitt said with a touch of acerbity in his voice.

"Easy, Jack," Troy said softly. "G2 doesn't assume. Norman is human. He forgot."

46

"I expect you're right, old boy," Moffitt said quickly. "But at least he didn't forget to provide them. He just forgot to tell us."

"Hey, Sam," Tully flung over his shoulder. "I'm hungry. We haven't eaten since morning and we sure as shooting got no rations. Did those G2 guys pack us a picnic lunch or did they slip up?"

Troy had a sinking feeling in the pit of his stomach, part hunger, part apprehension. Food hadn't been mentioned and he was afraid this was plain oversight. The idea of another twenty-four hours without eating did not appeal to him. They had water and they could manage, but there would be unnecessary discomfort. "Is there a flashlight in the front seat?" he asked.

"A big one," Hitch said, handing back a six-celled flashlight with a large head.

Troy swept its bright beam over the bags and cans of water and gas on the floor of the back seat. There was no picnic hamper, no package of sandwiches, no cartons of C rations. G2 had forgotten to provide food and it angered Troy.

"We'll go through a village," he said irritably. "If we can't buy some eggs, we'll run over a chicken."

"Nuts," Hitch said. "They give us booze but no food. I don't even have any gum."

"I don't believe Norman would be guilty of such a lapse," Moffitt objected. "Perhaps he did forget to tell us about the grenades but they were here. Every detail has been attended. Norman was extremely careful to keep everything in keeping with the character of the Enna brothers. Traveling about a savage land, you would expect them to be accompanied by small luxuries, potted eel, artichoke hearts, champagne."

"Cut it out," Hitch complained.

"You might expect it, but where is it?" Troy snapped.

The car came to a gentle stop and Tully turned. Even in the muted light of the transparent night, it startled Troy to have a fierce, mustached stranger looking at him from Tully's head. "What's wrong, Sol?"

"It don't seem right to me either," he said. "This car's got a trunk behind. There's usually things in trunks."

"Like tools," Troy said gloomily.

47

Nonetheless, when Tully, Hitch and Moffitt had stepped from the car, he stood hopefully, first scanning the surrounding country. Tully had parked on the top of a dune. The night sky was light blue and the desert floor all about was ultramarine with black patches that marked the pockets. About half a mile ahead on either side of the trace, the ragged silhouettes of a handful of palms marked an uncharted oasis. Troy examined it carefully and studied all the shadowed hollows for movement. The Enna brothers seemed alone under the vast vault of the evening sky. He turned, hanging over the tonneau and looking down. Tully had unfastened the metal straps that secured the lid of a large trunk mounted on a rack at the rear of the car. He was standing with both hands on the lid. Hitch was scowling, the creases between his eyes looking like grease marks on his face. Moffitt's teeth showed whitely in an amused smile.

"I'm afraid to open it, Sam," Tully said, looking up at Troy.

"Go on, Sol," Troy urged. "Be brave."

"If there ain't food in there, my stomach won't live with me no more," Tully groaned. "It's been complaining it ain't being treated right ever since we hit those Ay-rabs."

"Come on, Sol, open," Troy said encouragingly. He chuckled softly.

"Oh," Tully moaned. "There goes my belly again, just a-growling awful."

Troy grinned as Hitch pushed Tully out of the way and threw back the lid. Troy beamed the flashlight into the trunk.

"Will you give a look at that!" Hitch gasped and Tully stuck his head and both hands into the trunk. He pulled away, straightening and triumphantly holding aloft a cloth-wrapped Westphalian Kugel ham that must have weighed twenty pounds.

Troy played his light forth and back over the assortment of cheeses and sausages, tins and jars of gourmet food. A wicker hamper stood at either side of the trunk. "See what's in the hampers," he said.

One contained dishes, cutlery, and cooking utensils. The other was filled with bottles of Asti Gancia Spumate wine and Liquore Galliano packed in straw.

48

"I was rather certain Norman would do nothing to diminish the image of the Enna brothers," Moffitt said; a trifle smugly, Troy thought.

Tully was hugging the German ham and chanting: "Between the lips and over the gums, look out stomach, here ah comes."

"*Ricottari!*" Troy said in a severely disapproving voice, scarcely suppressing a chuckle. "Watch your language, Sol. That's no way for a *capo* to talk."

"Hey, that's kosher, boss," Tully said, surprised.

"Put back the ham, shut the trunk," Troy said. "There's a small oasis just down the trace. Get the car in the trees and we'll take a break for dinner."

Tully nosed the car well off the trace into the palms on the south side of the track. There were perhaps a dozen trees here growing about a brackish waterhole and they afforded good cover. Troy had once more observed the desert all about them and was satisfied they were alone, but when Moffitt and he stepped from the car on opposite sides, each left his violin case behind and carried a bare tommy gun.

Tully already had the lid of the trunk up and his hands were inside. "Look, Sam," he said and the front of the trunk dropped down to make a table.

Troy beamed the flashlight on the store of provisions as Moffitt and Hitch came around to the back of the car. No one spoke for a moment as the light dazzled on three hams, canned Norwegian herring sprats, anchovies and sardellen, Beluga caviar, Carciofini, half a dozen sticks of sausages, cans of smoked sturgeon, crabmeat, lobster, shrimp, pate de foie gras, smoked oysters, pickled lambs tongue, pickled walnuts, pickled nasturtium pods, hearts of palm, pearl onions, olives Italiene, and cheeses—Roquefort, Liederkranz, Camembert, Edam, Swiss. There was Major Grey's chutney and Bercy sauce; French dressing and Russian dressing; tins of Melba toast, crackers and cookies; a tin of Danish butter; a five-pound can of coffee; a dozen cans of condensed milk; fresh oranges and limes, and a string of garlic.

"I wonder who gave up his ration points," Hitch said at last.

"Don't anyone ever say anything against G2 again," Troy said fiercely.

"Look what I found," Tully said. He'd been rummaging in the hamper with the dishes and brought out a Sterno stove. "Anyone for coffee? There's a pot in here."

"Your G2 isn't infallible," Moffitt said with mock bitterness. "They forgot the tea."

"These are props for Dietrich's benefit," Troy said, grinning with the others. "But it wouldn't look right if we hadn't touched the stuff. Brew up a pot, Sol, open some cans and slice the ham. I'll go back on the dune and stand watch until the buffet is spread."

He started to move away. Moffitt gripped his arm tightly. "I wouldn't go just yet, Sam," Moffitt whispered. "We're going to have company." He nodded his head toward the dune.

Creeping down the trace without lights was a slant-nosed Jerry Volkswagen patrol car. Troy could see the outlines of four Jerries in the car and three of them were hanging over the sides with their machine guns ready.

7

Tully went wild. The thought of a battle raging about their cupboard must have been what set him off. The coffee pot clattered on the table formed by the side of the trunk. He growled like a maddened animal, low in his throat, and plunged for the back door of the car. With two Jerry stick grenades in his hands, he spurted from the oasis into the desert, circling wide to intercept the Volkswagen. He looked like a Balkan anarchist with his handlebar mustache, curly black hair and civilian clothing.

Troy flipped his tommy gun off safety and started after him. Abruptly he changed course and ran toward the patrol car in a crouch along the side of the trace to cover Tully with diversionary fire if necessary. He didn't think the Jerries suspected they were in the oasis and swore under his breath at Tully. If he'd used his head and stayed put, they could have ambushed the patrol and caught the Volkswagen in cross fire. The Jerries either had seen the car from a distance or found the tracks on the trace and followed them. The enemy patrol was deep in Allied territory. There was only one explanation. They were here on Dietrich's orders to get the Rat Patrol if the Arabs failed. One, the 109s; two, the Arabs; three, this patrol. No matter how he tried, he couldn't read coincidence into these facts that spoke with guns. Troy dropped to his hands and knees and crept toward the slowly approaching Volkswagen. The Jerries were wary, the men in the back seat peering intently at each side of the track, and the man beside the driver leaning out around the windscreen to inspect the way ahead.

The car was about three hundred yards away when it stopped abruptly and the man beside the driver lifted his light machine gun as he twisted to the side. Behind him, the man on his side had his weapon to his shoulder. They had seen Tully. Troy, on the opposite side of the trace, jumped up, ripped off three fast bursts and fell to the ground. In the moment the startled Jerries hesitated, Tully threw a grenade. It was short by a good fifteen yards, but the flash and concussion of the explosion blinded the Jerries and threw their aim off. Three of them fired but the bursts were wild. Troy rose on one knee, fired two more bursts and flattened on the sand. A moment later the Volkswagen blew apart in a flaming blast that threw firelight all the way to the oasis and hurled chunks of twisted metal everywhere. Troy hugged the desert floor until the ammunition in the car stopped popping, then pushed to his feet and brushed the sand from his suit. Norman needn't have worried about its looking new, Troy thought as he walked cautiously toward the burning wreck. Not that it made any difference now. They weren't going anywhere except back to Bir el Alam.

Tully came out of the night onto the trace and the two of

51

them halted well away from the blaze. The patrol must have been carrying an enormous reserve of gasoline from the size of the fire, Troy thought. Of course they were carrying a load of gas. They hadn't known how far they'd have to chase the Rat Patrol.

"What'd they have to come along for?" Tully demanded bitterly, breathing hard. The fire threw sparks onto his contact lenses and his dark eyes appeared to glint angrily.

"They'd picked us up and were following the tire treads," Troy said. "We'll have to get out of here. If there's another patrol car, they'll see the fire." He laughed without humor. "It wouldn't make any difference if it were Allied or Jerry. We'd have a job explaning ourselves, the way we're rigged out."

"Damn them crazy fools!" Tully exploded. "They spoiled our supper."

"I guess we spoiled theirs," Troy said dryly.

They turned and walked quickly back to the oasis. The Hispano-Suiza was on the trace, the trunk strapped shut. Hitch was at the wheel and the motor was idling. It would be foolhardy to continue on the mission, but they couldn't turn back until they were certain the way was safe.

"Drive fast without lights for about ten miles," Troy told Hitch as Tully and he swung into the car. "Then pull off the trace into a wadi and we'll have supper."

"Going on with it, Sam?" Moffitt asked quietly as the car eased ahead in second gear.

"I've got to think about it, Jack," Troy said, looking over the back of the touring car at the fiery wreck. It was a lonely pyre. If there was a second Jerry patrol car it was ahead, waiting to intercept them.

He settled back, alone in the corner of the back seat. They had their orders. If he returned to Bir el Alam, he'd be disobeying them. Under the circumstances, he could explain their failure to carry out the assignment, but the Rat Patrol had never turned back from a mission. They could return and request a new plan but Norman and Bernard had probably gone back to Cairo. They could go on, improvising a new plan of their own. Or they could carry out the original plan, assuming that the three events of the day had been unrelated although that seemed entirely improbable.

52

The moon, a huge white globe, sat on the horizon now, diffusing its bright illumination over the already translucent desert. Moffitt's—or rather, J. Enna's—features were clearly visible. His mustache was the handlebar type of the first generation Mafia. He looked like a ruthless pirate with his black hair blowing in the wind kicked up by the speeding touring car. It was a shame that such a carefully prepared cover should have been broken by Wilson's prattling.

Troy's stomach was stewing when Hitch ran the car off the trace, driving a mile through dark valleys to hide the tread marks, and finally stopped in a wadi well protected by high dunes. Troy told Tully to use the Sterno stove and brew a pot of coffee. He took a cup to the top of a dune to stand guard and think. He had no appetite for the ham or cheese and sausage Tully was heaping on the plastic plates from the hamper. What they did from this point on was his decision to make. He went over the events of the day again to see whether he could add them together and get a sum that was mere chance.

It was true the Messerschmitts came over the Allied position regularly on strafing runs. If the fighters discovered a B-25 on the ground or taking off, of course they'd hit it. Arabs were predators who prowled the desert and lurked on the fringes of towns and camps waiting for their victims. If a band happened upon a lone civilian car, or a lone military vehicle for that matter, they would pounce upon it. But how could he explain the Jerry patrol car deep in Allied territory? It was possible that Dietrich or some other Jerry commander had sent a patrol behind the lines to harass and destroy in the same fashion the Rat Patrol operated and coming on the track of the Hispano-Suiza or seeing the car at a distance, had decided to investigate.

It was shaky rationalization, Troy admitted glumly. Could he read in any positive conclusions that Dietrich was not aware of their mission into the events? If the fighters had been ordered to shoot down the B-25 they would not have given up so quickly. If the Arabs had been told to kill the Rat Patrol, they would not have fired at the car from a distance. If the patrol car had been after the Rat Patrol, the Jerries would not have followed the tire tracks, but would have swung wide ahead and ambushed them.

It was possible to make it come out like that. Maybe it

53

was stretching things a bit, but Troy didn't see that he had much choice except to take the possible and not the probable. Wilson had said the mission was vital.

Troy closely inspected the desert before he stood. Far in the distance was a small flame where the patrol car still burned. Otherwise the desert was quiet. Not even a jackal slunk across a dune or barked. He walked briskly over the dunes that embraced the wadi scanning the silvery sands and then slid into the valley where a blue flame flickered under a fragrant pot. Moffitt, Tully and Hitch watched him without speaking as he took a plate, speared a slice of ham, spooned some caviar on a round of toast and half filled his cup with sparkling Asti Gancia wine.

"Prèsto, mustachios," he said, cramming his mouth with Westphalian ham. "What you wait for? We got long way to go *stasera.*"

"Si, parone," Tully shouted.

Hitch yelped and smacked Tully between the shoulder blades. Moffitt's, or J. Enna's, eyes didn't twinkle but the amused smile was familiar even under the mustache.

It was strange that Troy had not noticed the others had been under a strain. Perhaps he had been too occupied with his own thought. It was as if suddenly a tension spring had been released. Hitch and Tully began horsing around, swaggering about the wadi with their violin cases. J. Enna leaned against the trunk-table that was loaded with delicacies. He twirled his mustache with a Continental flair but the smile lingered and was reminiscent of Sergeant Jack Moffitt, late of the Scots Greys.

"We're with you, Sam," he said quietly. "We were afraid you'd turn back."

8

The moon rode high and the desert was eerily washed with turquoise light when Hitch turned the big wheels of the Hispano-Suiza off the trace. Here, almost at the southwestern edge of the Cyrenaica peninsula, the track ran straight north to the ocean. Some fifty miles to the northwest, Wilson sat on the desert bed and looked up at Dietrich on the ridge. For almost the entire distance, Dietrich's southern flank was protected by a salt marsh. Directly south was the Great Salt Marsh, an enormous area two hundred miles long and a hundred and fifty miles wide, where nothing lived and there was no sound nor motion except the dancing wind dervishes. Between the marshes, a ridge of barren rock rose like the backbone of a dinosaur. It was one of the ribby outthrusts from this skeletal range that Dietrich occupied.

Although it was nearing twenty-two hours, Hitch had not needed to use his headlights. Troy was not certain whether this was to their advantage. While it was easier to run with lights, he did not like the idea of being visible for miles from both the land and air. There had not been further incident, however, after the encounter with the patrol car and Troy had dozed intermittently, relieved and easy in his mind now that the decision to go on with the original plan had been made.

When Hitch left the trail, Troy sat stiffly, straining as the desert cleats of the tires clutched loose sand. The car slowed perceptibly but not significantly and continued over the trackless desert at a steady thirty miles an hour toward the beginning of the stony highland. Within a mile, the sand began to show rock outcroppings and Hitch slowed to twenty miles an hour as he steered an erratic course between them. The land began to tilt and stones stuck knotty fists out of the sand. Abruptly, the car was above the desert on a sheer rock face that lay in slabs canted toward a ridge some one hundred and fifty feet high. Hitch stopped, and with the motor idling, he filled the radiator from one of the water cans in the rear seat. The engine had not started to heat. The night was cool and only tendrils of vapor lazed above the radiator.

"I'm going to use the searchlight, Sam," Hitch said over his shoulder as he moved the stick into position for low gear.

Troy could feel the transmission gears turning over as Hitch kept the clutch depressed. He'd told Troy what he was going to do, but he wanted approval. Troy would rather have continued without lights but one way was as bad as the other: use the lights and risk being observed; go on without lights and risk being hung up on a rock.

"You're the driver," he reminded Hitch.

The searchlight thrust its inquisitive finger up the rock-ridged incline, ran back to the car, swept the gray slabs of stone on either side. Hitch slanted the light across the hood so it touched the ground about ten feet ahead. He let out the clutch and steered the car across a flat slab of rock at a forty-five-degree angle to the right. He followed this outcrop for about fifty yards and stopped to explore a flat layer of stone that ran upward to the right. The searchlight traveled this stretch, then leaped on, climbing up a steep ramp to the top. The searchlight ran up and down this face of stone. Troy swallowed hard. He would hesitate to go up that sheer ascent on foot. He remained silent.

The car crept upward in a setback to the left without seeming to strain in low gear and the final ramp loomed straight ahead. Hitch stopped, aimed, gunned the motor and let out the clutch. The car started to crawl up the wall like a fly. The incline was so steep Troy felt as if he was lying on his back. He could not see the top of the ridge. All he could see was the bright night sky above him. If the tires lost their grip they'd crash to the bottom of the slope. He dismissed that thought the moment it flashed across his mind. The car lurched and they were on the top. A rending rasp scraped from the undercarriage and the car came to an immediate and abrupt stop. The back wheels were inches off the incline on the top. Hitch had shut off the motor, set the brake and he and Tully were under the car before Troy recovered. He and Moffitt hopped out and knelt on either side of the car peering under it. Hitch was inspecting the underside with the flashlight.

"We're hung up on the pan," he called. The flashlight beam probed. "It doesn't seem to be punctured on this side. Here, Sol." Troy saw him hand the flashlight around a flat-topped rock. In a moment the light beamed from the other side. It held steady in one position for several moments.

"It's not leaking," Tully called. "You stopped in time."

Hitch backed from under the car, stood and blew out his breath. He stepped to the back and glanced down the precipitous slope. "Only an idiot would drive blind up that," he said disgustedly and looked back at the car.

"What do we do?" Troy asked. The mishap annoyed him and left him feeling helpless but he was not angry. Hitch hadn't had a choice. He'd had to shoot over the top and he hadn't had a periscope. If it hadn't been for Hitch's immediate reaction, the pan would have been ripped off.

"We can't drive it off," Hitch said. "That'd take the pan. We can't lift it off. The car weighs about four tons."

"Can we rock it off?" Troy asked.

"Be the same as if we drove it off," Hitch said.

Tully and Moffitt walked around from the other side of the car. Troy lighted a cigarette and the four of them stood looking at the big powerful Hispano-Suiza, immobilized but not quite impaled.

"If we had a chisel and hammer, we could knock off the top of the rock," Troy said.

"It would take all night," Hitch said. "Besides, I don't think we have a chisel." He flung open the tool box mounted on the running board on the driver's side, turning the flashlight into it. "Hammer," he said, holding up a small sledge. "No chisel."

Tully moved beside him and started removing wrenches and screwdrivers. He laid an assortment on the running board. "Give me the flashlight," he told Hitch and started to crawl under the car. "Oops," he said, backing out and

57

standing. Tully was grinning, or rather, Sol Enna was smiling ferociously. "Better take care of the masquerade costume." He removed his suit coat and trousers and stripped down to his underwear. Troy saw he was still wearing GI khaki shorts.

"When you get dressed again," Troy said with a thin smile, "you better put on your pink silk shorts. Norman would blow a gasket if he knew what Sol Enna was wearing under his gabaradine trousers."

"I wish we'd only blown a gasket," Tully mumbled, crawling under the car with the flashlight.

"What do you have in mind?" Moffitt squatted and inquired.

"I'm going to take off the pan," Tully called. "Maybe I can slip it off when Hitch drives the car ahead."

"What are the chances?" Troy asked Hitch.

"Not chances, Sam," Hitch said with a grim smile. "It's our only chance." He was stripping down to his shorts. "I'll give you a hand," he shouted at Tully and turned to Troy. "You and Jack might as well take a bottle of wine and go smoke a cigarette. Right now you're useless."

The remark probably was true, but it irritated Troy. He walked away from both Moffitt and Hitch and stood beyond the hood of the car looking along the top of the ridge. It was broad and reasonably flat, jagged but passable with caution. Far to the south, the Great Salt Marsh was a spectral sea. To the north he could see the other marsh, Dietrich's marsh, glittering greenly in the moonlight. Abruptly he turned.

"I'm going to get some food and drink to carry in the car," he told Moffitt. "With the time we lose here, we won't be able to stop again until morning. If we do get moving."

Hitch gave him a Mark-Enna, dirty-dog scowl and dived under the car. Troy found a bare foothold behind the automobile and hung onto the rack as he unstrapped the trunk. The ham was on top and he tossed that into the back seat as well as a sausage, a good sized chunk of Swiss cheese, a tin of biscuits, a knife and four plastic cups. He tucked two bottles of wine under his arm, strapped the trunk shut and edged around to the side. When he'd deposited the bottles in the back seat, he thought briefly of getting out the Sterno stove and brewing coffee but rejected the idea. It was less than two hours since they'd had their supper. If Hitch and Tully got the car off the rock, they'd move right out.

Hitch rolled from under the car as Troy started for the rock to the side where Moffitt was sitting. "We're going to give it a try," Hitch said. "Want to bend over and give me the word if Tully sings out?"

"Sure, Mark," Troy said, kneeling. Tully was holding the loosened pan with both hands. Troy saw the front wheels being cramped to the right and the car edged ahead.

"Stop!" Tully shouted.

"Stop!" Troy repeated.

"What's the matter?" Hitch called when he'd set the brake.

"I can't slip the pan off," Tully called. "It's wedging in tighter. The rock will go through it."

"Just a minute," Troy said. He lay on his back under the car looking at the pan mashed against the rock. He rolled out and looked at the rear wheels. Although close to the edge, they had firm purchase on the stone. "Screw the pan back on," he bent and said to Tully. "Jack," he called to Moffitt. "Give me a hand."

"Of course," Moffitt said quickly. He walked over to Troy. "How can I do my bit?"

"We want some flat stones," Troy said, bending over with his eyes on the ground. "A couple about an inch thick and a couple about two inches thick."

"Right-o," Moffitt said, stooping immediately and lifting a thin slab. "Like this?"

"That's the ticket," Troy said, picking up a stone about the same size. "We'll cram these against the front tires and find two thicker stones."

By the time the two-inch stones had been laid in front of the first slabs, Tully had replaced the pan and was standing beside the car.

"Put it in low and gun it over the stones," Troy told Hitch.

There was a brief scratching noise of metal against the rock and then the tires mounted the stones. The pan cleared the rock as the Hispano-Suiza rolled free onto the ridge. Hitch set the brake and stepped out to get into his clothes.

59

"I guess that's why you're a sergeant, Sam," he said mournfully as he pulled his trousers over his shirt tails.

After Tully had exchanged his shorts for more suitable undergarments from his handbag and left his GI underclothes beneath a rock, they piled back into the car and moved on along the arm of stone. The searchlight stabbed the path ahead and the car dodged in and out of the slabs that jutted from the broad ridge. The bright night turned cold and Troy voiced no objections when Hitch and Tully complained bitterly at the inefficiency of G2 in failing to provide blankets. With only suit coats, they all were shivering.

At midnight, Troy checked the mileage with Hitch and found that despite the hangup on the rock, they had covered twenty miles since twenty-two hours. He wanted to be off the high thrust of land by daybreak, but with six hours to cover eighty miles, he felt safe in calling a break. Hitch stopped in an area near the middle of the ridge that was free of obstacles as far as Troy could see.

"We'll take half an hour," Troy told Tully. "Time enough for a cup of coffee to warm us up."

"It's colder'n a coon's nose at Christmas," Tully grumbled, taking the flashlight. "I wish we had Norman and Bernard in short-sleeved shirts with us right now." He walked to the back of the car. Troy heard the lid of the trunk go back and the side slap down. Abruptly there was silence. There was no sound of rummaging for the coffee pot and cups, the stove, the coffee can. Just dead quiet, as if Tully were standing motionless. Then Tully said, "Sam." His voice sounded weary and resigned.

Troy went to the back of the car. Tully turned the beam at the bottom of first one hamper and then the other. Both were well off the floor of the trunk. Tully lifted one of the hampers. Folded beneath it were two white wool blankets. Two more blankets were under the second hamper.

"We didn't lift out the hampers," Tully said. "We didn't notice they were riding high."

Tully and Troy each wrapped a blanket around himself and Troy carried the other two to Moffitt and Hitch.

"Things seem to be picking up a bit," Moffitt said with a J. Enna smile that lifted his mustache.

"Why didn't Tully find them before?" Hitch complained,

60

throwing the blanket over his shoulders.

"Why didn't you find them?" Troy mocked. "Your hands were as deep in that trunk as Tully's."

"Why didn't you?" Hitch demanded truculently. "You got into the trunk for the ham and wine when we were hung up."

"Because I was hanging onto a skyhook," Troy said and laughed. He looked around. The high land at the area where they had stopped was at least a mile across the hump before it sloped away to the sand that lay between the ridge and the salt marshes. It was level and unobstructed ahead and to the sides. They had taken the sensible course, he thought, and the only safe way.

"Sam. . . ." There was absolute horror in Tully's voice and it trailed off in a moan.

Troy, with Moffitt and Hitch at his heels, ran to the back of the car. Tully stood motionless as if he were paralyzed. The greenish cast of the moonlight made the terror in his face ghastly. He lifted his arm slowly, as if he were in a trance, and pointed. Troy heard a noise like the rattling of chains as he turned to look. He gasped and shuddered, and for a moment, like Tully, he was transfixed.

Converging from either side near the middle of the ridge were two columns of twelve tanks each. They were miniature tanks, about four feet long and two feet high, certainly not large enough to contain humans, yet they maneuvered with precision as they approached each other to within a distance of about three yards and turned sharply in a column two abreast. They crawled like lines of soldier ants and their continuous caterpillar treads ground relentlessly with a steady drone.

They were awesome little monsters, more dreadful than two columns of Mark IVs. The thought flashed across Troy's mind that these machines that could not possibly have human operators yet which performed with such military exactness were straight from H. G. Wells. The beastly little vehicles were driving for the car and the attack was terrifying.

9

A blast shattered the night and the flash from the explosion glared over the ridge. Another detonation followed immediately and then there was a nerve-jangling series of them, as if sticks of dynamite had been fused together like firecrackers in a string. The sky was stabbed with blinding lightning and buffeted with violent thunder. The rock trembled, the sky shuddered and all was quiet, although a fire raged where the Hispano-Suiza had been parked for the coffee break.

"You can slow down now," Troy said to Hitch. His voice rasped and there was a quaver in it.

The car had been at least a mile away when the first explosion crashed against the ridge and the shock waves slammed their eardrums. They had recovered from the near panic that had seized each of them at first sight of the unearthly weapons, banged the trunk shut and sped away in a headlong dash from disaster.

"Okay to stop?" Hitch asked shakily. "I got the jitters."

"Stop, shut off the motor, set the brake," Troy said. "We'll pass around the flasks."

He glanced ahead as the car stopped, saw the path was clear ahead before Hitch switched off the spotlight. Turning, he studied the blaze and saw no figures moving about it nor in the moonlight beyond.

"What were they, Sam?" Tully asked as Troy slumped back in the corner of the seat. Tully's voice was hoarse and his face seemed bilious. "What kind of things was after us?"

"Just doodlebugs, Sol," Troy said, but there wasn't

much reassurance in his voice. "Nasty little remote-controlled, self-propelled mines Jerry has devised. They ran into something or got out of control, piled into each other and blew up."

"Oh," Tully said. He didn't sound relieved. "I heard about them. I've never seen one before." He shook his head. "Don't want to see one again."

"Coming out of the night at you like that, unexpected, they jam you for a minute," Hitch said.

"I'm still shook," Tully admitted.

Moffitt handed each his silver flask from the handbags. "Jerry doesn't often use them," he said. "Actually, they're not a bit effective."

"Effective enough to have blown the car and us right off the ridge," Troy muttered. He was morosely silent for several moments. He gulped a swallow from his flask and said, "I think we'd better go back."

He stared sightlessly at the flask in his hand. He could feel three pairs of eyes on him but no one said a word.

"I've tried to explain away the other three attacks as unrelated events that just happened that way," he went on. "This doodlebug deal is too much. Dietrich knows our cover, he knows our route, when he doesn't get us one place, he's waiting for us down the road a piece."

"How could Jerry know precisely where we were going to halt for a break?" Moffitt asked quietly. "We hadn't even planned it ourselves."

"Whether or not he knew where we were going to stop," Troy said angrily, "he was there with those damned doodlebugs when we did stop."

"We happened to stop in a clear area where he was experimenting with the mines," Moffitt suggested.

"Rationalize! Call it coincidence! Say we were a target of opportunity," Troy said furiously. "The point is, Jerry saw us. He sent those doodlebugs after us. He had to be here on the ridge to do it. If Jerry didn't know about us before, he does now."

"Jerry may have seen the searchlight from below," Moffitt countered. "It doesn't follow that he saw us. He was below and knew simply that anyone up here in the testing area didn't belong to him."

"He was up here; is up here," Troy declared in a coldly

63

toneless voice. "He had to be up here to control and observe his mines."

"What do you imagine he saw from a distance?" Moffitt
asked with an irritating J. Enna smile. "A searchlight."

"And the outline of this car," Troy said curtly.

"Things look very different at a distance in the dark,"
Moffitt argued. Troy was beginning to be annoyed at his
persistence. "If he did see the car from a mile away, he
could not identify it in daylight."

"He could be damned suspicious," Troy snapped.
"Look, we've been attacked four times since yesterday
morning. Only a maniac would go on and bust into
Dietrich's camp throwing grenades and shooting."

"How would you return, Sam?" Moffitt asked. "Past the
Jerries with the doodlebugs? Past the patrol car and Arabs
we shot up?"

"How would you go on, Jack?" Troy said bitingly.
"Continue on the route where Jerry has us pegged? Walk into the next trap and let Jerry slam it shut? It isn't just
myself. I've got the three of you to think about."

"Oh, come now, Sam," Moffitt said. He sounded
disgusted and impatient. "You aren't going to start thinking about us at this late date."

"Knock it off, Jack!" Troy exploded. "It's idiotic to go
on with this cover. Everything indicates it's been blown. I
don't mind taking chances if there's one small percentage
that the risk will succeed. Only a fool delivers himself as a
sacrifice. We're not doing Wilson any good by getting captured and being shot."

"There is more than a small percentage in our favor,"
Moffitt insisted. "Jerry is going to have to explain that
fiasco with the doodlebugs. He does not know who we are
and I very much doubt that he will mention an enemy patrol that got away. We don't even know that he was attached to Dietrich's unit."

"It's all too iffy, Jack," Troy said. Moffitt was doing exactly the kind of thing he'd done himself earlier, finding in-
nocent excuses for the damning facts.

"A small percentage in our favor," Moffitt repeated
softly.

"Jack, you know I don't want to turn back," Troy said
irritably. He looked at Tully and Hitch, scrounged around

64

on the front seat. "What do you say, Sol? Mark?"

"Crawl back into that hole in the desert and twiddle our thumbs when we can wear civilian clothes, ride around in a Hispano-Suiza and gorge on truffles and caviar?" Hitch asked derisively. "You nuts or something?"

"You'll never stick a pig sitting in your kitchen," Tully said.

"It looks as if it's settled, Sam," Moffitt said. The only thing that pleased Troy was that Moffitt didn't smile.

Tully and Hitch handed back their flasks. Hitch stepped on the starter and the Enna brothers once more were on their way. Troy wished he could put some faith in all the spurious reasoning he and Moffitt had done. They were committed to their cover and their mission now. Once off the ridge they could not turn back. He voted the assignment the most unlikely to succeed of any caper they'd ever undertaken.

Hitch was not using the searchlight. Looking back, Troy saw that the fires from the explosions were dwindling. There still were no figures moving anywhere on the ridge. It was strange that no one had approached the blown doodlebugs to investigate. He tugged the blanket closer over his chest and settled comfortably back. The night air was sharp and clean in his lungs. Despite his apprehension, Troy dozed.

He awakened with a start to find the car had stopped. It was only Tully and Hitch changing places at the wheel. The next time he awakened, his stomach felt hollow. The touring car was poised nose down on a very steep decline. Moments later they were off the ridge and threading through a boulder-strewn slope toward the cactus-studded desert. Troy thrust his hand into his pocket for his lighter, flipped it against his wristwatch and saw by the hands of his synthetic diamond encrusted wristwatch that it was oh-four-hundred. The moon was down and the sky was opaque blue-black. Tully was using the searchlight.

"Hold on a minute," he said quietly to Tully. Beside Troy, Moffitt stirred in his sleep and settled back.

The car came to a stop and Tully turned, leaning his arm on the back of the seat. Hitch hadn't awakened during the descent and was snoring gently.

Troy stepped onto the running board next to Tully. "Put

the flash on the map and give me the compass bearing," Troy said. He looked over Tully's shoulder at the chart spread over the big steering wheel. Tully held the flash close to the map so the illumination was a small bright circle.

"We're here," Tully said, pointing. "Off the ridge, at the end and west of Dietrich's salt marsh, between his position and Sirte except about fifty miles or maybe sixty miles south of him. And about fifty miles west of him. The going may be a little rough, but it's mostly desert until we get near the coast. Then we're going to run into some more hills and ridges. Our course is due north with allowances for anything we have to go around."

"You've made good time," Troy said. "Get in the back and curl up. I'll drive until dawn."

"I can hang on a couple more hours," Tully said.

"Sure you can hang on," he said. He grinned but his face felt tight and he could feel the strain. "But if there's one thing I can't stand it's a sleepy cook and lousy coffee for breakfast. Now git."

"Gotcha, boss," Tully said briskly and flatly.

Troy stepped off the running board and Tully slipped out of the car. "There are times I suspect all the 'shine you ran wasn't in Kentucky," Troy observed dryly.

"Thet drawl is jest a lazy way a-talkin'," Tully said, and in the light from the flash, Sol Enna winked a dark eye.

Troy emptied three of the five-gallon cans of gasoline into the tank, filled the radiator with water, laid a stick grenade beside him on the seat and put the car in gear. Experimentally, he turned off the searchlight before he started. Even after his eyes had adjusted to the dark, he could not make out the shapes of the boulders and cacti ahead. He did not like the idea of driving behind the Jerry lines with the searchlight on but the alternative was worse. Headlights would be a dead giveaway that some kind of motor vehicle was behind them. The single spotlight could be mounted on anything from a motorcycle to self-propelled gun. A Jerry patrol wasn't likely to fire without investigating.

The Hispano-Suiza was a surprising automobile. Big and clumsy as it appeared, it responded immediately and magnificently to the steering wheel and accelerator. The

66

engine hummed softly as Troy guided the car through the rocks and around the cactus. He was able to maintain a speed of between thirty and forty miles per hour with the spot beamed about fifty feet ahead of the car. Now and then when he entered a clear stretch of desert, he checked the compass and pushed the speed up to fifty. In two hours, they could be on the coastal highway driving east toward Dietrich's position. They'd be picked up as soon as it was light, if not before. They could be facing Dietrich across a breakfast table, sharing their sumptuous larder with him. It would give them extra time, providing their cover still held, but it also would give Dietrich an entire day to observe them in the full light of the blazing sun. Between eight in the morning and eighteen-hundred at night, whiskers would sprout. A look, an unconscious gesture escape to catch Dietrich's wary eye. It would be better if they arrived at dusk as he'd planned, Troy thought. They'd share a buffet supper with him and be in and out of his lines during the hours of darkness. If they were lucky.

They were well behind the Jerry lines in this desert area that was not a battlefield and there was no reason Jerry should be patroling so deep within his own territory, but Troy was not surprised when a light glared into his eyes and a voice harshly commanded, *"Stillstand!"*

Troy turned the wheels away from the spotlight as he let the car come to a gently rolling stop. He depressed the clutch and slipped the car into second gear. The stick grenade was in his right hand when he turned toward the voice. No choice, he thought bitterly. They were too far from the coastal highway to be discovered and taken in to Dietrich and their disguises had been ravaged by the night. The spotlight on the patrol car which was idling noisily was very close. Troy heard the footsteps in the sand on his side. He worked the steering wheel a little more to the right. He knew he could not handle the maneuver alone but there had been no movement in the car, nothing to indicate that any of the others was awake or aware of what was happening.

Suddenly he stepped on the accelerator, let out the clutch, hurled the grenade at the searchlight and turned the spot on it all in a swift, continuing motion. The car spurted away, three machine guns rattled, two bursts of enemy fire raked them, the grenade exploded in the sand, two more grenades blasted and the patrol car flamed and exploded. The Hispano-Suiza had leaped away but was rocked with the blast and was showered with sand. Troy spun the car around and the searchlight found a Jerry enlisted man with a light machine gun running away from the wreck. Before taking after him, Troy inspected the area around the blazing car. The others in the patrol apparently had been caught in the car. When Troy beamed the searchlight back, the running Jerry had disappeared. Gone to ground, Troy thought. They had to get him.

The light jumped from one clump of cactus to another as the car prowled the desert beyond the circle of light that spread from the fire. A volley spattered at them as the light struck a rock. Troy swerved and put the car behind the stone, keeping the spotlight on it. The Jerry scuttled around, firing burst after burst. Troy was relieved the man was firing. They could not have shot him if he hadn't and they could not afford a prisoner. The Jerry still was firing as Tully's machine gun cut him down.

"Now, Sam," Moffitt began as Troy sped away from the burning car.

"I won't say a word, Jack," Troy said. "We're in their territory. We've got to expect to run into them." Still, he wondered why the patrol should have been in this particular area at this time of the morning.

No one slept after the encounter with the patrol car. There was no indication that there was a second patrol, and after five or ten minutes the tension drained away. Troy lighted a cigarette.

"Anyone for ham and cheese?" Tully asked; hopefully, Troy thought.

"Wait until we stop," Troy suggested. "With what we have in the trunk, we might as well have a VIP breakfast."

Moffitt chuckled and Troy knew he was going to make some remark about the condemned man eating a hearty last meal. He'd had enough of that. "Knock it off, Jack," he said sternly.

"I only meant to ask, what is the plan, Sam?" Moffitt

said with mild surprise in his voice. "Are we going straight on?"

"No," Troy said. "I'd considered it and rejected the idea even before we ran into the last patrol. We'll hole up all day and go in late this afternoon. It's not just that I don't want Dietrich inspecting us in the daylight. Starting with the Arabs, we've left a pretty plainly marked trail. The longer the time lapse, the less chance of Dietrich connecting us with the two patrols and the doodlebugs. We'll ditch the grenades before we visit Dietrich."

"The pineapples have been handy little gadgets," Moffitt observed.

"Potato mashers," Troy corrected. "If you're going to use gangster jargon, you'd better be sure it's right. A GI grenade is a pineapple. The stick grenades have been handy, but they would be embarrassing when Dietrich goes through our stuff. He'll know about the patrols by then. We're going in clean."

They drove on wrapped in blankets and silence until the blue-black of the sky began to turn to gray and the landscape sprang into darkly silhouetted view. Troy switched off the light and pressed down on the accelerator. They flew past a native village, a dozen mud and wattle huts with goats and a few chickens contained in thornbush corrals. On a cactus prickling hill in the distance, Troy saw the high walls and flat buildings of an old French fort.

"Looks deserted," Hitch beside him commented. "That's a good place to hide out."

"It would be the first place the Jerries would look when they discover what happened to their patrol," Troy said.

"Not much other place to hide," Hitch said.

"It's rocky and there are ridges between the road and the ocean if I read the map right," Troy said. "We're going to hit the road, drive a few miles east until we come to a trail going toward the ocean that won't show our tire marks. We're going to find a gully or ravine and sweat it out. If we're discovered, I want to be on the other side of the road."

"Uh huh," Hitch said.

The terrain became rough and crimped, eroded hardpan and rock as they neared the edge of the desert plateau before it fell off into the sea. The car crawled out of a bar-

69

ren wash onto the grade. In the gray light just before dawn, it was deserted in both directions. The Hispano-Suiza rolled onto it in second gear. Troy shifted into high and pressed the accelerator.

"Keep your eyes peeled," Troy called. "I'm going to give it everything it's got."

The speedometer needle crept past seventy-five, touched eighty miles an hour. Troy suddenly realized that an Italian car normally would be gauged for kilometers instead of miles and wondered whether G2 had added yet another touch to authenticate their U.S. gangster backgrounds.

"Ahead," Hitch shouted. "About a mile. It looks like a track."

Troy slowed, touching the brake lightly. His speed permitted an easy turn onto the hardpacked clay and stone roadway that curled lazily in the direction of the Mediterranean. It probably led to a coastal village, he thought, driving fast until a ridge hid them from the grade. He slowed then, drove on another mile until he came to a stretch of flat dun-colored rock. He drove across it until he came to a gully with a hard clay bed, braked and looked back. No tread marks on the windswept stone showed that an automobile had come this way. He nosed the car onto the hardpan and followed the bed until he came to a steep-sided ravine that twisted out of sight. He backed into the declivity, around a bend and they were hidden except from the air.

"If only we had a camouflage net," he said wearily, turning off the motor. "I'd feel reasonably secure."

"One in back," Tully said laconically. He stepped from the car, stretching, grinned and drawled: "It's under all the groceries. You didn't think G2 would forget a simple little old thing like a camouflage net, now, did you?"

70

10

Nothing annoyed Herr Hauptmann Hans Dietrich quite so much as to be interrupted at breakfast and his staff, including also Lieutenant Doeppler, was aware of his fondness for tranquility with his sausages. Doeppler actually was not on the staff but performed line duties as the need arose for expendable personnel. Doeppler was a quartermaster temporarily at a loose end since all of Dietrich's stores had been abandoned at Sidi Abd and there was a completely efficient Sergeant Kauderwelsch permanently stationed on the ridge, who provided not only clothing, fuel and transportation, but an occasional dozen fresh eggs or case of brandy. Doeppler had been exposed to a smattering of training in infantry, artillery and engineering before he'd been shunted into a supply post. The varied experience, far from recommending Doeppler to Dietrich, explained why he bungled every task he undertook.

"What is this matter that cannot wait until the *Frühstück* is completed?" Dietrich harshly asked Doeppler. The lieutenant stood in front of Dietrich's long solid table in his tent. His small, close-set eyes stared straight ahead, not at Dietrich but above his head. This was a habit of his that never failed to infuriate Dietrich. He pushed aside his plate of fried eggs and *Wurst,* not yet touched by his knife.

Doeppler wet his lips with the tip of his tongue and began to speak, chewing his words without moving his heavy jaw. "I am sorry to report that all of the two dozen mines you sent me to test last night have regrettably been destroyed," he said mechanically.

"What!" Dietrich gasped and his stomach turned sour. "That cannot be."

"*Ja, Herr Hauptmann,* it is a thing that cannot happen," Doeppler said without expression, eyes still fixed on the wall of the tent behind Dietrich. "All the same, they blew themselves up."

Dietrich was physically ill. From the moment the Arabs had revealed that there was a British twenty-five-pounder in the Allied camp, he had wrestled with the near insurmountable problem of dealing with the long-range weapon. In an inspired moment, he had remembered the robot mines he had discovered stockpiled in the arsenal on the ridge. He had sent Doeppler with a patrol far from the position to run them through a series of operational tests. It had been his intention to slip Doeppler and a squad out the safe passage to destroy the gun in the pit with the remotely controlled mines.

"The entire two dozen of them?" Dietrich asked faintly.

"*Ja, Herr Hauptmann,*" Doeppler confirmed.

"It is a great misfortune," Dietrich said despondently, "but it is well we discovered in advance that they were not dependably operational."

"The robot mines were themselves completely operative," Doeppler said stoically.

"What is that you are saying?" Dietrich demanded, eyes going cold as his stomach grew warm with wrath.

"The robot mines functioned with an exactitude that was a pleasure to observe," Doeppler reported. "It was not until they encountered unexpected obstacles that they destroyed themselves, and that of course is the way they were designed to perform."

"What obstacles?" Dietrich asked furiously. "How did it happen? Commence with the beginning and finish it to the end. Tell me exactly what occurred."

"As you wish," Doeppler said. "It was in this fashion. Twelve of the mines I placed under the supervision of Sergeant Schmitt and sent him across the ridge to the foot on the other side of the clear area. I remained on the north side at the bottom with twelve of the others. At a prearranged time, we started the robots up the slope, removing ourselves at a distance in the event there was a malfunction."

72

"Go on," Dietrich said tersely. Of course Doeppler would remove himself to a distance. Once the mines had been set in motion, he undoubtedly had leaped into one of the trucks and driven off a mile.

"The robots performed well on the slope. When they reached the top of the ridge and were all lined up, twelve on each side, they stopped as we had arranged."

"Yes?" Dietrich said sharply. "And then?"

"I observed the beam of a powerful light traveling on top of the ridge."

"A searchlight on your testing area!" Dietrich exclaimed. "Who was it? What did you do?"

"Immediately, I called Sergeant Schmitt and informed him of the intrusion," Doeppler said, not without pride. "Together we returned to the bottom of the ridge, each on his own slope, and executed an explicit maneuver. We despatched the robot mines in a column of twos after the intruder who had stopped upon the ridge. The intruder was the Rat Patrol."

"The Rat Patrol," Dietrich said weakly, feeling as if he were crumpling in his canvas camp chair. "Are you certain?"

"Of this I am certain," Doeppler said firmly. "With my own eyes I saw them, first from a distance and then from closer up. When first I noticed, one jeep was leading the other with a powerful light. The second jeep followed close behind. Next I saw them from the top of the ridge where I hastened when the robot bombs exploded. They had driven away in the same formation with the leading jeep directing its searchlight along the ridge."

"What was the Rat Patrol doing more than fifty miles south on the ridge?" Dietrich pondered aloud. "Only a few hours earlier the Arabs saw them in the camp."

"That is what I asked myself," Doeppler said, "but they had as much time as I to reach the ridge. It is possible they were suspicious and followed the Arabs."

"The Rat Patrol within our lines?" Dietrich shuddered at the thought. He said without conviction, "That is impossible."

"Of course, Herr Hauptmann," Doeppler said, "but there they were on the ridge. They were aware of what we were testing and set a trap. The searchlight was to call out

73

attention to them. They wanted us to set the robot mines after them so they could rob us of their usefulness. The Rat Patrol stopped long enough on the ridge only to plant mines of their own or to erect a barrier into which the robots would crash and detonate themselves. It was impossible to determine which after the explosions."

"Why did you not call the robots back when you saw what the Rat Patrol was doing?" Dietrich raged.

"It was not known they were aware of the approaching robots," Doeppler said. "Until the last moment, they waited, then they leaped into their jeeps and sped away. Not until it was too late and the robots were piling one upon the other in terrible destruction was it apparent what they had done."

"Doeppler, I am certain that in some way you are at fault," Dietrich declared sternly. "In which direction was the Rat Patrol traveling?"

"The Rat Patrol fled to the west," Doeppler said.

"The Rat Patrol did not *flee,*" Dietrich said, exasperated. "If they drove west on the ridge they are behind our lines engaged in another mission against us. Already they have destroyed the only two dozen robot mines we possessed. Who was on patrol duty in the far western sector last night?"

"*Leutnant* Stengle," Doeppler answered promptly. "He has not seen them, I am certain. I have questioned the radio operator and there has been no report from him. Of course, he would have called in a message if the Rat Patrol had passed within his sight."

"No report!" Dietrich thundered. He pushed the table away from him, upsetting his coffee cup, and ran from his tent bareheaded. "Kloake!" he shouted as he rushed toward the communications truck.

A fair-haired, cherub-cheeked boy poked his head from the back of a canvas-topped truck parked just beyond the tent. Rosebud lips smiled innocently at Dietrich.

"What was the hour and nature of the last report from Stengle?" Dietrich asked tensely.

"At midnight, *mein Hauptmann,*" Kloake said cheerfully. "It was a routine position report. There has been nothing since that hour."

"He should have returned at oh-six-hundred," Dietrich

said tightly, rage now turning to icy calm. "Why was I not advised?"

"First you were asleep and then you were at your breakfast," Kloake shyly observed.

Dietrich groaned. "All right," he said feeling completely frustrated. "First, call me up Stengle on the wireless. Second, raise Mueller. He is on a reconnaissance patrol within the enemy lines but I must talk with him. *Versteh*?"

"*Ja, mein Hauptmann,*" Kloake said with a hasty bob of his blond head. "It shall be done."

Dietrich lit a cigarette and paced outside the truck, ten steps forward, about face, nine steps back. Doeppler stood stolid and motionless. *Was zum Teufel Hölle,* what mischief was the Rat Patrol up to now? Already they had tricked Doeppler into destroying the one weapon capable of penetrating the enemy position and knocking out the British twenty-five-pounder.

After five minutes, Kloake poked his head from the back of the truck. "It is regrettable but I am unable to receive an answer," he said. "There is no signal from either of them."

"What was Stengle's position at his last report?" Dietrich asked.

"The bearing or in plain language?" Kloake asked.

"Plain language," Dietrich snapped. "It's for Doeppler."

"A moment, *mein Hauptmann,*" Kloake said. His head disappeared and thrust back out almost at once. "*Lieutenant* Stengle reported from seventy-eight kilometers to the west and sixty-nine kilometers to the south."

Dietrich swung on his heel and confronted Doeppler. "Did you register the position?"

"*Ja,* seventy-eight kilometers to the west and sixty-nine kilometers to the south," he parroted.

"Very good, Doeppler," Dietrich said with heavy sarcasm. "Now, take a halftrack with a full crew and a patrol car with a driver and two men in addition to yourself. Go directly to this position of Stengle's last report. If you do not find him, or what is left of his patrol, there, search until you discover what has happened to him. Maintain contact by wireless on each hour. When you have found Stengle, and I fear for the worst, check each wadi and place of concealment between him and the road. The Rat Patrol is somewhere in concealment waiting for the dark."

"But, *Herr Hauptmann*," Doeppler started to protest.

"Yes, yes, you have been on duty all night with no rest," Dietrich acknowledged. "I do not need to remind you that a soldier is never off duty, and unfortunately there is no one else I can spare."

Doeppler drew himself up stiffly, saluted and silently turned on his heel.

"Keep trying to raise Stengle and Mueller," Dietrich told Kloake and strode to his tent. He snatched his peaked Afrika Korps cap from his locker, swept the binoculars from the table and walked rapidly to the flat rock next the halftrack. Ignoring the Allied armor, he focused directly on the camouflage net stretched over the pit which the Arabs had reported contained the heavy artillery piece. Although Doeppler had been positive enough in his identification of the Rat Patrol, it was always possible that the bumbling lieutenant had met with some misadventure which he blamed upon the Rat Patrol. The net was stretched tight and there was no one in the area. Now Dietrich inspected the camp meticulously, starting with the V of Sherman tanks. The crews were out of the slit trenches and were swarming over the tanks. Dietrich frowned. It could be only normal maintenance or it could be preparation for action.

The crews for the halftracks seemed more than normally busy with their weapons. Dietrich caught a fleeting glimpse of the American Colonel Wilson entering his headquarters tent and lifted the glasses through the supply trucks to the airstrip. A large work detail moved in a line slowly down the runway compacting it with tampers. There had been men on the runway before and after the landing and departure of the B-25 bomber the day before but he had paid scant attention to them. He worried now at the large work force obviously engaged in more than routine upkeep of the strip. Could it mean that B-25s were going to bomb the ridge from only a few miles away, refueling and stocking their arsenal there?

Once more, he inspected the Allied camp yard by yard. Nowhere was there visible sign of the Rat Patrol. Doeppler actually had seen them, Dietrich admitted reluctantly. Sergeants Troy and Moffitt and Privates Hitchcock and

76

Pettigrew were somewhere within his lines. As he turned slowly to return to his tent, he thought he glimpsed a white object moving and raised the glasses once more. The American Colonel Wilson in his flamboyant white varnished helmet had left his quarters and was walking toward the supply trucks. At the camouflage net that covered the pit, he paused for a moment, stepped to the end, flapped back a small section of the netting and crawled into the position.

Dietrich felt the perspiration burst from his scalp at his hair roots. If he'd needed confirmation of the Arab's report, Wilson was providing it. He was checking the twenty-five-pounder, gloating over his weapon, chuckling at the way he would sit back out of range and pound the slope and ridge until he'd cleared a pathway for his armor. When Wilson crawled from the pit and walked on toward the runway, Dietrich returned at once to his tent. He wrote several urgent messages. First he requested not two ineffectual Messerschmitts but a flight Heinkel He 111s to bomb the enemy camp. Then he requested long-range 88 mm. FLAK 18s to reach the pit with the British twenty-five-pounder. Third, he requested a case of brandy. Something very definitely was in the air.

He imagined he actually could feel the weight of the messages when he carried them to the communications truck. Somewhere between the coastal road and the ridge that ran between the marshes, the Rat Patrol had crawled under a camouflage net in a wadi and were waiting for darkness to creep out, ready to pounce on an unsuspecting patrol or slip into his depots and dumps and blow them up. They would discover the reinforcements that had come in, including the four tanks that had arrived the night before. They would observe the emplacement of his artillery.

When he returned to the tent to wait for the answers to his messages, he was drenched with perspiration, although it really still was cool so early in the morning. He sat at his table clenching his fists. He could not wait for Doeppler to reach Stengle's last position and confirm what Dietrich already was sure had happened. Dietrich had to find and kill or capture the Rat Patrol now. He called in Kraemer and ordered him to take three halftracks and search every wadi and building from the coastal road to the ridge on a vector five miles wide on either side of Stengle's last known position.

Wilson had just returned from his morning tour of inspection when Corporal Locke had burst into the tent with a message form folded in his fist. His face was expressionless but his eyes were shining with excitement. He thrust the message at Wilson who took it silently and frowned. It was another Eyes Only communication which Locke had decoded. He remained in the tent while Wilson read the message, waiting to see that the form was properly destroyed. Damn it, Wilson thought irritably, why does the man have to assume that I'll be careless?

The message read: *Special ordnance arriving your position ten-hundred tomorrow. Essential that testing be completed within twenty-four hours. Repeat, utmost security must be enforced.*

He dutifully burned the form and Locke left the tent. When Wilson turned his head, he saw that Peilowski was watching him with a look of concern in his eyes. Locke, Peilowski, even the Rat Patrol treated him as if he didn't know enough to come in out of the rain. His gray eyes glinted and he had opened his mouth to chew out Peilowski, but his self-discipline took over. The truth was, he admitted, he was worried about the Rat Patrol. And now this message made it appear he had sent them on a useless mission. By the time they returned with the information, if they did obtain it and managed to return, the ordnance man and his missile-launcher would have come and gone.

"Has the detail completed work on the runway?" he quietly asked Peilowski.

"It could be used by a C-47 right now," Peilowski assured him with the air of a man who has completed a difficult task ahead of schedule. "There's still a crew out there tamping. They'll be done today."

"Good," Wilson said, and then suddenly and inexplicably sorry for his first sergeant, he tossed Peilowski a harmless bone. "It will be in use tomorrow. Full security measures starting at oh-six-hundred."

"Yes, sir!" Peilowski said smartly. Wilson was certain

78

that if Peilowski hadn't been seated he would have saluted.

Picking up his white varnished helmet, Wilson slipped the strap under his chin and stepped from the tent. He walked briskly around the tent and started toward the strip. When he came to the camouflage net, he stopped, glancing at the OFF LIMITS signs and smiling. Each man of the Rat Patrol in his own way was brash, undisciplined as far as authority was concerned, decidedly an individual who refused to be recast in a military mold. Not the type to make an officer's life easy. Yet he had no better soldiers in his command.

The net had been stretched tight again following the capture of the Arab and the rat hole would not be occupied again until Troy, Moffitt, Hitch and Tully returned. The substitute Rat Patrol had departed from the camp by the simple expediency of depositing the distinctive headgear in the cave with the jeeps and returning to their units. He had planned to have the four men on hand and in evidence for another day but he hadn't been able to tolerate Merriam's brutality. The Lord knew what difficulties he'd create for Troy if the impersonation were permitted to continue.

Wilson started again for the strip and hesitated at the ramp end of the hollow. He not only disliked Merriam, he distrusted him. If the man had copped Troy's bush hat, there'd be a brawl when the Rat Patrol came back. Merriam would be lucky if he escaped with only a broken arm but then Wilson would have to discipline Troy. The CO peeled back a corner of the net and slipped down the ramp. The three distinctive headpieces and Tully's conventional helmet were where they should be, on the front seats of the jeeps. Wilson blew out his breath in relief and looked about the quarters of the Rat Patrol. It really was quite cool and comfortable here beneath the desert, he thought. The two jeeps stood ready for action at either side and the space between was packed and clean. He imagined it was a good deal more bearable in this cavern during the hot days than under the canvas at his HQ.

He crawled out, replaced the netting and strolled through the supply trucks to the runway. The work detail had compacted the strip for more than half its distance and the C-47 should have no difficulty in making a smooth landing.

79

Back in his tent again, Wilson considered his problem. Without information from the Rat Patrol, he would be at a loss to know where to concentrate the area saturation fire. given him. Well! He stood abruptly and crashed his fist on the table. There was one sure way to find out where some of the enemy's guns were located. He turned to Peilowski whose eyes were startled.

"We're going to attack the ridge today," he said in a clear, strong voice. He felt happy and excited. "You want to see some action?"

"You're going through that minefield?" Peilowski asked hesitantly and his jaw was slack.

Wilson laughed. "I'm going to send a dozen tanks with all guns blazing up to the edge of the field. I hope we can trick the enemy into opening up and reveal his emplacements. Come along in the staff car to observe and chart them."

This time Peilowski did salute. Despite his pudginess, he managed to leap to his feet and bring his hand slapping against his forehead. "Yes, *sir!*" he said enthusiastically. "I always did want to see some active duty."

11

Dietrich swallowed the responses to his three wireless requests but found he was unable to digest them. One, no bombers available; request denied. Two, no FLAKs available; request denied. Three, brandy? You cannot be serious; request denied. He could not say that he was disappointed because he really never had been hopeful. A year before, perhaps at least one of the requests would have been confirmed, but with the Allies now hammering at the Afrika Korps on every front, it was simply do the best with what you have.

He drew the canvas camp chair to the table and lifted the metal cover on the luncheon plate which Grosse had just brought. Although the events of the morning had been upsetting, he had not eaten any breakfast and he was hungry. Aromatic steam curled from the plate and his eyebrows arched as he wrinkled his forehead in surprise. Two thick rib cutlets embraced half a dozen small boiled potatoes that were coated with melted butter. The chops undoubtedly were goat—or at the very best, kid—and the butter undoubtedly ersatz, but the potatoes looked genuine and the appearance of the plate was appetizing. He knew the coffee would be good. The incomparable Sergeant Kauderwelsch somehow managed to obtain whole beans which he ground with no cereal additive. A large porcelain mug beside the plate was filled to the brim and fragrant tendrils rose from it. He removed the war from his mind and sat down to enjoy the meal. The fork with a juicy slice from the cutlet was halfway to his mouth when firing broke out.

As he reached for his cap, his mind was busy cataloging the weapons. He identified the whoosh and hollow burst of the mortars, the sharp rattle of the machine guns, the high-pitched whine of rifle fire piercing the heavy sounds, the shattering boom of the 75 mm. cannon and the screaming of the rockets. It sounded as if the ridge had exploded. He also detected the detonations of 75 mm. shells that were shuddering against the slope. They were similar to the shells fired by his own 75s, but not quite the same. The Allied 75 mm. shells seemed to slam and burst with a slapping detonation. Wilson had launched his attack, he thought, and waited for the awful blast of the twenty-five-pound shells from the gun howitzer in the pit.

Field glasses thumping against his chest, he ran toward the flat rock that overlooked the valley from a position beside a halftrack. The halftrack was gone and he remembered he had sent Kraemer with three halftracks to assist Doeppler in the search for the Rat Patrol. The firepower from four halftracks withdrawn from battle! he thought and his head ached dully. In the place where Kraemer's halftrack had been emplaced, an ox of a man was standing, feet well apart as if to brace the massive body against the

81

shock of the blows from the shells. His back was to Dietrich and under his short-sleeved shirt his shoulders bulged like animal haunches. Hands were to his face, cupping field glasses. It was Major Haussie, the artillery officer who commanded the guns on the slope and ridge but who temporarily was under orders from Dietrich. In North Africa, the tanks of the Afrika Korps came first.

The valley and the slope were enshrouded with a gritty mist of sand and dust that roiled to the ridge itself. The opaque clouds reverberated with each shell blast. Dietrich lifted his glasses, but it was impossible to see the attacking force through the turbid air or see the results of the firing from the slope and ridge. The Germans and the Allies slammed shells blindly at each other.

"Have they used the twenty-five-pounder yet?" Dietrich asked. He dropped his glasses and wiped the abrasive particles from his eyes. Already, perspiration was making muddy tracks on his cheeks.

Haussie let his glasses fall against his great belly and bent his head down to Dietrich's. When the face was so near that Dietrich could see the little purple veins under Haussie's skin, the major blinked surprisingly clear blue eyes solemnly and rumbled, "Do they possess a twenty-five-pounder, Herr Hauptmann?"

"They have a British twenty-five-pounder howitzer concealed in a pit," Dietrich yelled.

"You know that this is so?" Haussie said.

"This is a fact that has been observed," Dietrich answered. "Soon they will be using it." His throat was raw from talking above the noise and he stopped to swallow. "With what are they attacking?"

"With a V of Sherman tanks they came at us," Haussie thundered. He seemed to have no difficulty raising his voice above the roar and crash of battle. "They have not for one minute let up since but we are holding them off."

Abruptly Dietrich gripped Haussie's hammy shoulders with both his hands, horrified at the thought that had erupted in his mind. *"Schwachsinnige!"* he raged at the top of his voice. "Call off the guns. Cease the firing. The tanks cannot cross the minefield without blowing themselves up. From where they fire they are not within effective range. Dunderhead! They are drawing your fire to get the range of the emplacements for the twenty-five-pounder. Cease firing!"

"*Herr Hauptmann!*" Haussie exclaimed, and his face grew so livid his veins disappeared. "I am your superior."

"Major Haussie," Dietrich said harshly. "As long as my armored column of the Afrika Korps remains at this position, I am in charge. You will command the guns to cease firing. That is an order."

He turned brusquely and marched to the communications truck. There had been two position reports from Doeppler and an observation on the weather. The wind was blowing.

"Kloake," Dietrich called as he approached the truck. The boy's head appeared between the canvas flaps. His eyes looked frightened. "Anything more from Doeppler or Kraemer?"

"*Nein, mein Hauptmann,*" Kloak said nervously. "What is happening with the battle?"

"Nothing, not a thing at all. Soon there will be no more firing," Dietrich assured him. Already the guns were falling silent; by banks it seemed. "It was a mistake and no one was hurt. Have you been able to raise Mueller?"

"I am happy it was a mistake and no one was injured," Kloake said with a timid smile. "Also, I regret that all I receive from Lieutenant Mueller is silence. But I shall persevere, sir."

"That is good," Dietrich said, voice softening as he looked at Kloake with an almost paternal feeling of responsibility. Perhaps it was necessary to draft up the boys so young, but why didn't they keep them for the defense of the Fatherland, close to home? "I shall be on the rock observing if I am not in my tent."

"*Ja, mein Hauptmann,*" Kloake said. He sounded grateful. Dietrich felt a lump gathering in his throat and walked away quickly.

He went to the rock. Haussie had left and now the firing was sporadic. It fizzled out during the next five minutes until there was only an occasional rifle shot from some embittered enlisted man who found expression and release in his weapon. The firing from the Shermans became desultory and then they were silent. The clouds that had puffed from the desert and the slope still obscured the Allied tanks but in the stillness, Dietrich could hear the clanking of their treads. By the time holes were torn by the breeze in the tawny veil that hung over the valley, the Shermans were halfway back to their formation in the Allied lines.

As he had discerned at once, the entire maneuver had been another American deceit. Tricky Yankee, descendant of *Jan Kees*. Fortunately, he'd been in time to stop that mutton-brained Haussie before the enemy was able to get the range for the twenty-five-pounder.

The wind had blown the dust out toward the sea and now Dietrich could see the tanks moving into their original positions, hatches flying open, crews tumbling out. Trucks began to shuttle between them, unloading shells. The camouflage net still was tightly in place over the pit, he saw, and at the airstrip the work crew had almost completed tamping the entire length of the runway. That was something else again to corrode his mind with worry. First there was the twenty-five pounder. Now the runway that was being prepared to receive something formidable.

He neither marched nor strode to his tent. He walked deliberately, and although he was erect with his shoulders thrown back, he felt as if he were slouching. He sat at his table and absently lifted the fork to which the bit of meat still clung. It was cold and had a decidedly goaty taste. The ersatz butter had congealed on the potatoes. The coffee was tepid and grit gave it substance. He pushed the cup and plate away and poured a glass of brandy. He had no appetite anyway.

Kloake ran into the tent and halted at attention. *"Mein Hauptmann,"* he said breathlessly, "Lieutenant Doeppler reports he has found the patrol of Lieutenant Stengle."

"Yes?" Dietrich waited patiently but not hopefully for the rest.

"He reported the patrol car had been destroyed—he thought by a grenade. It had burned itself out with three men of the patrol. The fourth, an enlisted man, a Corporal Verkehr, had been killed outside the car behind a rock where he had fired until the drum of his MG42 was empty."

Dietrich nodded his head sadly. Stengle had been outmaneuvered by a standard Rat Patrol tactic with the two heavily armed jeeps. "Verkehr, Corporal," he made a note.

"I shall see that he is awarded the Iron Cross, Second Class, posthumously. He was a brave man to stand alone against the Rat Patrol."

"Lieutenant Doeppler reports also that the wind increases its strength and visibility is limited," Kloake said. "Although there are no tracks to follow he will continue with the search for the Rat Patrol."

Dietrich shook his head wearily. If there were a sandstorm it would undoubtedly sweep into his position from the west and he could expect the Rat Patrol to ride into his camp on the tail of it.

Peilowski was sweating. He always perspired freely—to Wilson's intense annoyance—but now there was a reason for it and the sweat crawled down his cheeks and dripped from his jowls. He stood in front of Wilson's desk, clinging to a clipboard which held a paper on which a scaled map of the slope and ridge had been drafted. His moist cheeks were pale beneath the sunburn and the board shook in his hands.

"You did not mark a single position?" Wilson repeated frostily. The generous response the 75s had received from the ridge had pleased him beyond all expectations.

"You couldn't see where anything was coming from in all that dust," Peilowski mumbled.

"But surely you observed the first rounds that were fired," Wilson said evenly although his mind was frigid.

"I saw them all right," Peilowski blurted. "The whole hill was firing at us from everywhere at once. I like to hit the floor."

"Wasn't there anything that you could chart?" Wilson demanded.

"Well, I know where what was," Peilowski said.

"You know what?" Wilson asked incomprehensibly.

"I know what is where," Peilowski said. "First, above the minefield, there's machine guns and some riflemen. Then, halfway up the hill, there's mortars. On top, 75s and, I think, some rockets."

"Yes, you're quite right," Wilson said acidly. "I was aware of the disposition." He sighed heavily. "I'm afraid we shall be compelled to arbitrarily select an area to saturate."

"Yes, sir," Peilowski said promptly. "I guess that's what we'll have to do."

In spite of himself, Wilson smiled. He really shouldn't be too stern with Peilowski. After the first rounds he himself had been unable to locate the emplacement of the weapons. He supposed the best target for the missiles would be the minefield itself. Lacking the knowledge he hoped the Rat Patrol would bring back about the safe passage through the mines, he would be forced to direct the missiles on the minefield to clear a path for the armor. This meant his tanks would be assaulting the fortified ridge under direct fire from emplaced artillery. Casualties would be heavy.

A scuffle outside the tent interrupted Wilson's thoughts. He glimpsed whirling robes, bare brown legs, faded GI fatigues. Arabian invective shrilled in discordant, nerve-rasping cries. Wilson jumped from his chair and ran outside. Merriam, the former MP who had impersonated Troy, was wrestling with a small Arab in a ragged, soiled robe.

"You again?" Wilson said sharply. "What do you do, set snares for them?"

"When I see one sneaking around camp, I grab," Merriam said sulkily. He had one of the Arab's arms twisted behind his back. The man's other arm hung limply. "Maybe I should look the other way."

"Of course not," Wilson said, immediately sorry. "Bring him in." He went back into the tent and sat behind his table.

"I guess I shouldn't of bothered you, at that," Merriam said, shoving the Arab into HQ. "You warned him. You told him the next time he'd be shot."

Startled, Wilson examined the prisoner. He recognized the pocked face, the darting bright eyes of the native who'd been trapped in the net the night before. "Get Kalmuk," he told Peilowski. "I want to know why this man returned."

"I come to see you, *effendi,*" the weasel-faced Arab said in broken but understandable English.

"You speak English!" Wilson was astounded. He tried to recall what had been said in the Arab's hearing. He did not think anything of importance had been disclosed. Angrily he said, "Why didn't you tell us you spoke English?"

"I am treated bad," the Arab said and his eyes burned resentfully.

"Why did you come back?" Wilson asked.

"I have a thing to say," the Arab said. He jerked his head to the side, glaring at Merriam. "I talk when he let go."

"Release him," Wilson said to Merriam. "He came voluntarily. I don't think he'll bolt."

Merriam dropped the Arab's arm; reluctantly, Wilson thought. The truck driver suddenly seemed uneasy. He's concerned with what the Arab will tell me, Wilson decided.

"After I am here, I go with two friends to the camp of your enemy," the Arab said.

"Why?" Wilson asked coldly.

"We think we can sell story of what we see," the Arab said.

"Information about this camp?" Wilson asked.

"Yes."

"Did you?"

"No." The Arab's eyes were filled with wrath. "They treat us worse than your man. I do not understand what they say, but they beat us and beat us. My friends cannot move today."

"How did you get into the German lines?" Wilson asked.

"That is what I come to tell you," the Arab said craftily. "There is a way. They do not know it. You pay for this?"

"Didn't the Germans ask how you got into their lines?" Wilson asked suspiciously.

"We say we ride from west, no one stop us. You pay, I show path they not know."

"Yes," Wilson said. He did not trust the Arabs and had never dealt with them. He knew they peddled information to the Jerries. Perhaps he had been wrong. A trail into the enemy position not known to the Jerries would be invaluable. "I will pay you one hundred silver dollars but only after you have pointed out the trail."

"You are kind, *effendi*," the Arab said. He swung suddenly, half facing Merriam, and spit at his feet. Turning to Wilson again, he said, "Who I show? He?"

Wilson started to assure the Arab that it would be an officer who would treat him well when an idea flashed into his mind. Merriam needed to be disciplined. Brutality could not be tolerated.

"Yes," he said with a thin smile. "You will show him. You will be taken to a place to stay until it is dark and given food. This man and three others will go with you and you will show them the trail." He looked sternly at Merriam. "You will report to me at oh-nineteen-hundred with Corporal Heath and the other two who were with you on the Rat Patrol. When the Arab has shown you the path, you will scout it to the Jerry perimeter and observe the emplacement of their weapons." Looking back at the Arab, he said, "All you need do is show them the path. Return and I shall give you the hundred silver dollars." He glanced again at Merriam. "If the Arab tells me you have mistreated him in any way, you will stand court martial. Do you understand?"

"Yes, sir," Merriam said bitterly.

"You are very kind, *effendi*," the Arab repeated and Wilson thought he actually looked grateful.

12

An insufferable racket like the rasping of a thousand files against loose tin awakened Troy and he scrambled to his knees on the white blanket. His first glimpse of the three wild-haired strangers with bristling mustaches lying beside him shocked him and he dived for his submachine gun, but he was laughing softly as he came up with it at his hip. These men were his brothers. The Enna brothers. And the big old Hispano-Suiza touring car with them in the ravine was their car.

The screeching had awakened the others and they all

were sitting up. Their coats, trousers, shirts and ties, which they had carefully shaken and brushed, were neatly folded on the seats of the car and they had slept in their weirdly assorted shorts. Troy's were uncomfortable slithery silk, but at least they were white. Moffitt's shorts were the best of the lot, a very fine Egyptian cotton, but even concealed by trousers the color was enough to abash any self-respecting GI. They were cerise. Moffitt himself had named the color. Troy had called it cherry red. Hitch's shorts were a polka dot affair and Tully's were nylon and not pink, as Troy had predicted, but mauve, again, according to Moffitt, although they looked light purple to Troy. For a moment they disregarded the shrieking in their ears and sat staring at each other, then all burst out laughing.

"We'll have to ditch the shorts before we go back to camp," Troy said.

"Party pooper," Hitch accused.

"What's the buzz saw cutting?" Tully asked.

"It's a sandstorm, I think," Troy said, glancing at the camouflage net. It was rippling but they weren't getting the full force of the wind in the ravine. "We'd better have a look."

Carrying tommy guns, they trotted around the bend in the deep ravine to the dry bed. It was hot but the sky was hazed. Troy scrambled up the eroded claybank on the other side with the howling of a storm ringing in his ears and the fine reddish yellow sand flung out from its fringes stinging his face. The others stood beside him watching an enormous wall of burning, swirling sand more than two hundred feet high boiling through the desert on the other side of the road more than five miles away. It was sweeping westward away from them and it was not a mere sandstorm, it was a *Ghibli*. This was the desert wind that blew the year around, erratic, wild, unconquerable. The sand it churned so savagely blinded and suffocated. The *Ghibli* was a killer.

Troy searched the grade more than a mile away, saw nothing moving on it, and glanced at his watch. It was fifteen-thirty. He skidded down the embankment to the dry bed and looked at Moffitt, Tully and Hitch critically as they tumbled down and joined him. Hitch's face was stubbled with reddish whiskers. Tully's chin was a palish contrast to his black hair and Troy supposed his own contrasted too. Moffitt's beard was bluish-black. He was the only one of them who could escape detection if he didn't shave.

"Another hour, by the time we move out, we should be able to see the sun again. I think we'd better shave, get something to eat and be ready to shake it."

"Right-o," Moffitt agreed. "Nothing appeared to be traveling on the road. Do you suppose we'll have to drive to the perimeter unescorted? We don't have the password, you know."

"We'll be picked up," Troy promised, a little grimly. "Just hope the cover holds."

Back under the camouflage net, Tully unstrapped the trunk, dropped the front and lighted the Sterno stove on it. He pawed through the hamper that contained the picnic set, cutlery and pans.

"All right," he said at last. "It ain't here. Them G2 guys ain't so smart; they slipped up. They forgot a tin basin to wash and shave and soap and towels."

"Use one of the pots for shaving water," Troy said. "Put on a pan to heat. We can manage washing from a water can. We don't need towels but soap we do. I don't think they forgot."

He unzipped his handbag and opened the toilet kit. There was soap and shaving cream as well as toothpaste, toothbrush and a razor. The soap and toothpaste had been used. But he could find no towel in his handbag. It didn't make any difference personally. He could use a shirt tail or let the wind and sun dry his skin, but he did not think G2 would forget a towel for each of them. The basin? No oversight. The Enna brothers were city-bred. They wouldn't have thought to bring one along. But towels they would have carried. Troy grinned. He opened the outside flap to the compartment containing the flask, removed it and reached to the bottom. He brought out a rolled linen towel. "We're set," he said over his shoulder. "Jack, you first. Then Sol, myself and last, Mark. Shave it close."

Hitch looked balefully at Troy.

"Now, Red," Troy chided.

"Nuts," Hitch said.

"This is going to blooix up the coffee," Tully said, placing a pan with an inch of water in it over the flame.

"Can't be helped," Troy said. "We'll drink a bottle of wine. We'll be more in character if we go in smelling boozy. Who wants what for lunch? We haven't made an impression on the ham and cheese."

"Do we have to have ham and cheese?" Tully asked. "Can we have anything we want? Maybe this is the last we get to eat this stuff. Maybe Dietrich will grab it."

"That is possible," Troy admitted. "Go ahead, look over the assortment, take your pick. There's enough to feed an Army anyway."

Tully, already at the trunk, preempted first choice. He examined the stacks of exotic delicacies for a long time, finally turned to Troy and shrugged. "I'll stick with ham and cheese, toast and butter," he said. "There's none of this other stuff that's fit to eat. That fish egg jam last night was spoiled."

Hitch was scowling. "This is cockeyed," he said. "Who's to eat lamb's tongue and nasturtium pods? The other cheeses and the sausages are okay but what's the point? I'll go along with Sol."

"You know, ᴏ̶ ̶ boy," Moffitt said, tugging the J. Enna mustache thoughtfully, "our brothers have something there. I wouldn't mind a bit of chutney but nothing else tempts me."

"Cheese on ham, chutney side, coming up," Troy chanted. "I'm with you but I'd like my coffee. Sol, let me have the pot."

"You can't build a fire, Sam," Tully said. "There'd be smoke and anyway, there's no wood."

"Just let me have the pot and the can of coffee," Troy said patiently.

Moffitt chuckled. "Don't know why they couldn't have remembered tea," he said, "but I'll help with the coffee. You'll want stones."

Troy took the coffee can and pot, searching along the edge of the ravine until he found a crevice that was heaped with drifted sand. He scooped the sand in a high mound and placed the stones Moffitt brought on either side. Then he took a can of gasoline from the car, saturated the sand with it, filled the pot with water and eight heaping tablespoons of coffee and touched a match to the sand. There was a whoof as the sand burst into flame. When the gasoline-impregnated sand was burning with a blue fire, he placed the pot on the stones and grinned over his shoulder at Tully.

After they'd washed in tepid water, they shaved, using the mirror on the back of the car's searchlight. By the time Troy had added gasoline twice to the sand-fire and the coffee had come to a boil they all were ready to eat.

"I've been thinking," Troy said slowly as he piled a buttered round of toast with ham, cheese and chutney.

"Did it hurt?" Hitch asked innocently.

"For that corn, I'm glad I've been thinking what I've been thinking," Troy said, unruffled. "We don't know how much cover we've got left, but Dietrich's going to be suspicious of everybody who comes along. If we'd come in here clean and easy, it would have been one thing. The way things stand, he's going to suspect us because there are four of us."

"What are you thinking, Sam?" Hitch asked warily.

"Three of us go in, one stays here. If the rest of us aren't back in twenty-four hours, he tries to get through to take the word to Wilson."

"Who stays here?" Hitch asked bluntly.

"You," Troy said. "Moffitt, Tully and I will go in."

"Why me?" Hitch asked angrily.

"Tully can't swim," Troy said. "You may have to go back along the coast and swim around Dietrich's ridge. He'll have the beach patroled."

"All right," Hitch barked. "Tully goes in. But why Moffitt and you? Why can't one of you stay here?"

"Because we outrank you, Sonny," Troy said with a fast smile.

"That's no reason on a job like this," Hitch ranted. "There isn't one of you can handle a garrote the way I can. It isn't fair. I made the biggest sacrifice."

"Sacrifice?" Troy questioned.

"My hair," he said. "I'm shaved bald."

"We're all shaved bald," Troy said.

"But my hair was red," Hitch wailed.

"Do you think it's going to grow back green?" Troy asked, holding back a smile.

92

"They even dyed my eyebrows black," Hitch moaned. "They're going to look pretty fancy when they start growing out red at the roots."

"Eyebrows don't grow," Tully commented. He was having difficulty hiding the grin under his mustache. "Not one hundredth of an inch a year."

"So I got to go around with a bald head and black eyebrows until the dye wears off," Hitch said despairingly.

"The dye is more or less permanent, I understand," Moffitt said. The lenses concealed the twinkle Troy knew was in his eyes. "It's some new aniline compounded with a vegetable extract, I believe. Very popular with middle-aged ladies."

"See what I mean, Sam?" Hitch cried. "I'm ruined. You got to give me this last chance for the supreme sacrifice I made."

"You look all right to me," Troy said heartlessly. "You can just go on being an Enna."

"Why not just you and I on this mission?" Moffitt slyly asked Troy. "The two of us can handle it."

Troy nodded. "Okay, Sol stays behind to sympathize with Mark."

"I can't drag him if I've got to swim for it," Hitch said.

"*Rattos!* I give you the *pernàcchia!*" Tully stuck out his tongue and loosed a resounding Bronx cheer. "Among you, I am the only *pezzinorante.* You would go in with the *lupara* and every *tedesco* would have your number. My knife is silent."

"Huh?" Hitch said. "What'd he say?"

"Quite literally, I believe it ran something like this," Moffitt said, laughing aloud. " 'Rats, I give you the raspberry. I am the only executioner among you. You would go in with a shotgun blasting and all the Jerries would be on your necks.' "

Troy glanced at his watch. It was nearing sixteen-thirty. "Pack up, get dressed, let's roll." He stood without looking at Hitch.

"All of us?" Hitch asked, plaintively hopeful.

"All of us," Troy growled. "Maybe, if Dietrich is suspicious, he'll figure we couldn't be the Rat Patrol because we'd never do such a stupid thing as all four of us

93

come in." He looked up. "Give me a hand with the net, Jack."

When they'd folded the net, Troy removed half a dozen cans of herring, crabmeat and shrimp, an Edam cheese, a tin of crackers, one of the Italian sausages and a bottle of wine from the trunk. He wrapped the net around them, found a nook near the end of the ravine and buried the cache under a cairn.

"There's a survival kit for someone," he said. "I hope none of us has to use it."

It was a somber note on which to end the horseplay, but from now on business was deadly serious. After the series of attacks and encounters which had beset the mission from the start, he was filled with misgivings which neither Moffitt's reasoning nor his own rationalization could brush aside. When they all were dressed, he gave each a rapid, visual inspection. He had vetoed the suggestion of clean shirts and the suits were sufficiently rumpled to support the story of a long trip from Tunis. Their freshly shaved faces would be grimed with dust and streaked with sweat after a few miles. The disguises were intact. They looked like a murderous gang from a Grade-B movie. If the cover hadn't been blown, Troy believed they had a fifty-fifty chance.

"You pass," he said, facing Moffitt, Hitch and Tully. "How about me?"

"Sam Troy would shoot you on sight," Moffitt said, "and ask who you had been after a bit."

They checked their tommy guns, placed them in the violin cases and laid them on the seats. Troy ejected the clip from the Browning automatic pistol, ran his thumb over the cartridges, snapped them back into the butt and shoved the gun into his belt. Tully took the knife, a thin-bladed, needle-pointed stiletto, from his handbag and slipped it through the loops of his pants behind his belt. Hitch sulked because he had no garrote.

When the radiator had been filled with water and the tank with gasoline, Tully slid into the driver's seat and the Hispano-Suiza crept in second gear out of the airless ravine, along the baked dry bed, up the incline and over the hot smelling stone to the winding trail. No Jerry patrols roved the road and when Tully had turned the car onto it, he fed it gas until it was soaring over the scorched land.

94

The *Ghibli* had blown out of sight and the haze had dissipated. The lowering sun burned at their backs and soon Troy was sweating in his suitcoat.

Abruptly Tully called back, "Halftrack and scout car about a mile ahead. Do we pass or stop?"

Troy saw the dust trailing over the grade in the distance. He tried to think like Sam Enna. The American gangster and Sicilian black marketeer would be arrogant. His business was with the head man, Captain Dietrich. He would disdain anyone else. The Jerries would have to stop him.

"Barrel on," he called to Tully. "Let them do the stopping."

The car plummeted ahead and shot by the clumping halftrack and rackety Volkswagen showering them with dust and pebbles. Troy waited for a shell from the halftrack to sing over their heads but there wasn't even a burst of machine gun fire. He looked back. The Jerry vehicles were hidden by the dust.

"They aren't going to make it easy for us," he shouted, smiling wryly. "Okay, Sol. Pull over to the shoulder and stop. We'll wait for them."

13

Doeppler kicked his legs straight out, parade-style goosestep, when he marched into Dietrich's tent. He 'heiled' to Dietrich's apathetic acknowledgment and stood at attention. His face was laminated with layers of sweat and dust but despite his grubby appearance his little eyes that were set too close to the bridge of his nose managed to convey an impression of suppressed excitement.

Dietrich looked at him with jaded eyes and shuddered.

On the table before him was a cheese souffle. It was fluffy and golden brown. The airy masterpiece towered a good two inches above the rim of the casserole. A plate of toast was beside the souffle. Melting butter, ersatz but satisfactory on hot bread or toast, was dredging the slices. Coffee steamed in a porcelain cup. He had not eaten all day and he was hungry.

"Won't it keep, Doeppler?" Dietrich asked limply.

"I regret to interrupt your meal, *Herr Hauptmann*," Doeppler cackled as if his throat were clogged with dust. "The matter I wish to report is of supreme urgency."

"Only your report that the Rat Patrol had been captured would justify this intrusion," Dietrich said, but there wasn't much starch in his voice. The day had been trying. "Did you take the Rat Patrol prisoners, Doeppler?"

"I captured four Americans, *Herr Hauptmann*," Doeppler said stiffly.

"The Rat Patrol?" Dietrich said sharply. "Don't play games, Doeppler, don't try to be cute." He leaned forward but fell back again at once. "Of course they are not the Rat Patrol or you would have said so. Who are these Americans you have captured?"

"They are civilians," Doeppler said. "I think they are musicians. At least, each has a violin."

"So what are you doing, bringing me a stringed quartet to play for my supper?" The magnificent omelette was sagging sadly in the middle. "How did you capture them? Where did you capture them? What are they doing here in our territory?"

Doeppler frowned slightly, cracking the paste on his forehead. Dietrich thought that all of a sudden the lieutenant looked queasy. "They came flying up behind us like the *Ghibli* which nearly trapped us in the desert. They were driving a large touring car. It was on the coastal road. I stopped them and took them prisoner."

"Very astute of you to take them prisoner," Dietrich commented dryly. "And what were these four American civilians doing, flying like the wind on the coastal road?"

"As you know, I do not speak much English," Doeppler said. "They kept repeating '*Herr Hauptmann Hans Dietrich, Herr Hauptmann Hans Dietrich.*' I gathered they wished to see you."

"Astute *and* perceptive of you, Doeppler," Dietrich murmured.

"Thank you, *Herr Hauptmann,*" Doeppler said, gratified. "Do you wish to interrogate them now?"

The omelette had collapsed. It lay dejected and defeated below the rim of the casserole. A yellowish, waxy film covered the sodden toast. "By all means, Doeppler," Dietrich said. "Bring in your captives. We must not keep them waiting."

"*Ja, Herr Hauptmann.*" Doeppler saluted, about-faced and goose-stepped importantly from the tent.

Dietrich was only mildly interested in the four American musicians. When Doeppler had mentioned 'four Americans,' he had been alert immediately thinking the Rat Patrol had attempted some new deception. He had dismissed the thought at once. The Rat Patrol and he were too well acquainted for them to attempt tricking him even in disguise. He could not imagine what four American musicians could be doing within his lines. They probably were from a camp show unit and had somehow wandered through the lines. It was strange they should ask for him by name and he wondered how they knew it, but this evening he honestly did not care. His stomach protested mightily at the indignities it had suffered and all he wanted was to be left alone to eat.

Four men sauntered casually into the tent although Doeppler was guarding them closely from the rear with a Schmeisser machine pistol. Each of the men carried a violin case. They all had the same unruly black hair, dark eyebrows and hard brown eyes and fierce mustaches. They were dressed expensively and atrociously. One, a broad shouldered brute, smiled whitely to show a flashy gold tooth.

"I thought you said American, Doeppler," Dietrich said disgustedly. "These men are macaroni."

"The passports are here, *Herr Hauptmann,*" Doeppler said, a trifle officiously, Dietrich thought. The lieutenant spread four green booklets on the table before him. Dietrich leafed through the passports, scanning them, lifting his eyes only briefly from the photographs to the faces and not really identifying anyone, noting the visas. The names were Sam, Jack, Mark and Sol Enna, brothers apparently; same address on North Rush Street, Chicago, Illinois; departed for Italy by way of Mexico, November 22, 1940; visas for Spain, Algeria and Tunisia.

Dietrich addressed the affable scoundrel with the ostentatious gold tooth. The man also wore a large diamond on the little finger of his left hand. "Which of these," he said in English, waving his hand over the passports, "is you?"

"Sam, Captain, Sam Enna, that's me," he said breezily. He jerked his thumb at the other three, who stared fixedly and unsmilingly at Dietrich. The men made him feel uncomfortable. "These, *mi fràtelli.*"

"Yes, your brothers, of course," Dietrich said, sorting Sam Enna's passport from the others. He examined the photograph and looked back at Sam. He glanced at the photographs in the other passports and this time located the owners. "Remarkable family resemblance. According to these passports, you are citizens of the United States. This is correct?"

"Well, yes and no, Captain," Sam said airily. "We're born there all right, North Rush Street, Chicago, U-es-ay, like it says in the books. Things got hot and we had to scram. In case it hasn't registered, them little books is phoney as a three-dollar bill. Laid out a grand per copy in old May-he-co but the info is legit. What the hell, Cap, when you gotta go you gotta go, and the cops was breathing down our neck. So back we come where the old man and old lady is from, Enna, Sicily. That's right, Cap, even got a town named for us."

"The lieutenant reports you asked for me by name when you were captured," Dietrich said.

"Captured!" Sam reacted violently. He wrenched at his hair with both hands and pounded the table with his fists. He shouted furiously, "Who says we was captured? That punk *bastardo* of a looey? I ought to of shoved a shiv in his gullet. He was poking along in that tin can and we passed him up like yesterday. By the time we got stopped to ask him how to get here, he was so far behind it took half a hour for him to catch up. We followed that *lattaio* here."

"Just a moment, gentlemen," Dietrich said and glared at Doeppler. "You may leave, Lieutenant," he said. "Report to the duty officer. Inform him you have been ordered to relieve the regularly assigned officer of the guard tonight."

"*Ja, Herr Hauptmann,*" Doeppler croaked. The palm of his hand shot out. "Heil Hitler." He marched mechanically from the tent.

"Now," Dietrich said in English, studying each of the Enna brothers in turn and coming back to Sam. "You are Americans of Sicilian ancestry who left the United States under doubtful circumstances on forged passports in 1940. What are you doing here and what possible business could you have with me?"

"Just a minute, Cap," Sam said and his gold tooth gleamed. "We got a good reason for coming to see you. It took a lot of trouble and we drove all the way from Tunis, but before we go into that, I see we busted up your meal. How about we put on a spread, you know, like they say, turkey and all the trimmings? Maybe you like a change from this Army garbage, huh? Jack, Sol, Mark, lug in some stuff from the car. You got a boy, give us a hand, Cap?"

Dietrich gasped audibly. He'd seen characters like these in American movies before the war but he'd doubted their real life existence. Now he actually was confronted by four of them who claimed to have business with him. It was fantastic. He supposed they were sinister and the three who so far had remained silent looked villainous but Sam fascinated him. Gangsters, he thought and admitted he experienced a chilling thrill. Childish, he rebuked his emotions but his interest mounted. They were hiding from some—how was it called?—some rap and engaged in dealings on the Black Market.

"Grosse," he shouted, smiling at Sam. "He's my driver and orderly," he explained. "He'll assist your brothers. You have provisions of a sort stored in your car?"

"Provisions? Hey, that's rich," Sam exclaimed, slapping his thigh and bending over with laughter. "We don't exactly go for provisions, Cap. We carry a little something along for a snack, see? Yeah, that's what we got. A snack."

Grosse stepped into the tent and stopped short, staring at the four barbarians in civilian clothing.

"Four chairs, Grosse, and service for five," Dietrich said. "See if there is more coffee."

"Nix, Cap," Sam said, shaking his head and waving his

99

hands. "This is on us. We got java, we got a little stove. We're going to brew you up a cup that will carry you right back home. Tell your boy here to lug out what you was going to eat and help Sol and Mark and Jack get organized. You got some bread, we got the butter. It ain't necessary, we got toast and crackers but maybe you like bread with ham. You got some glasses, Cap? We got some Eyte bubble water. It ain't necessary, it drinks from a cup." He swung on the other three and waved both hands at them. "Move, move, *riccotari!* We're making a party."

To his own surprise, Dietrich found that he was amused and smiling. Sam's ebullience had caught him up and he was enjoying himself. "Grosse," he said, "clear the table, help the men remove what they wish from the car. Bring in chairs, the service, glasses, some bread. *Geh', Grosse, geh'.*"

Grosse had scarcely cleared the deflated souffle from the table when the piratical Sicilian-American named Sol bore an enormous Westphalian ham to the table and unwrapped the cloth to display the succulent red smoked meat. Mark and Jack Enna, trailed by Grosse, filed in and out of the tent loading the table with cheeses, seafood, garnishes, sausages, condiments, toast, crackers, cookies, fresh oranges and limes. Sol brought in a large can of American coffee, a coffee pot and a stove with a chemical burner. Grosse had an armload of sparkling Italian wine and liqueur.

Dietrich examined a few of the cans at random: smoked sturgeon, pickled lambs' tongue, hearts of palm. He glanced at the Liederkranz among the cheeses and at the ham that dominated the board. Not even in the peaceful days of abundance had he seen such a buffet. When the four brothers were lined together in the tent again and Grosse had departed for the chairs and service, he found his voice.

"You came bearing gifts," he observed. "I am certain the board groans but not my stomach. It is chuckling."

"There's more of the same in the car, Captain," Jack Enna spoke up. "We get hungry when we travel. We didn't bring gifts, but what we don't clean up tonight, you get to keep, see?"

Grosse came in with chairs, paused long enough to give

100

each of the Enna brothers a searching look and went out again. Dietrich smiled inwardly. He could well understand the man's curiosity.

Jack reached for a bottle of the sparkling wine. "A glass or two before we dig in, okay, Captain?"

"In a moment," Dietrich said. "In just a moment Grosse will have the glasses here."

He had only spoken the words when Grosse reappeared and placed five stemmed glasses on the table. He stared openly at Sam and Jack Enna.

When the glasses were filled, Dietrich lifted his to his guests. He was in rare good humor and kindly disposed to this band of cutthroats. "I do not know your business with me, gentlemen," he said and a smile touched his lips. "But may it be such that it can be successful."

"We'll drink to that," the one called Sol said and his mustache lifted when he smiled. The smile did not touch his eyes. They were dead as fish eyes.

Dietrich glowed as the wine effervesced on his empty stomach. He mellowed as he gorged. He was surfeited and warmly content by the time coffee and liqueur was poured. Mark passed around American cigarettes. The five of them sat about the table, sprawling in the camp chairs.

"I don't know when I've enjoyed anything quite so much," Dietrich said and sighed. "Now I suppose you will want to get, as I believe you say, down to brass tacks. I hope this business that has brought you here is something we can negotiate. Technically, since you are citizens of the United States, we are enemies although I imagine your present residence in Sicily could be considered a mitigating factor."

There was a soughing sound and a series of pops as several rockets launched flares. Outside the tent the flat white light made the acetylene lantern hanging above the table seem dim. Sam looked startled.

"Flares, to prevent an unexpected attack," Dietrich explained, amused, as Grosse stepped in and began to clear the table. He covertly examined the profile of each of the Ennas as he removed the jars and cans near him. The man's curiosity was one thing but this close inspection was another. Dietrich was becoming annoyed.

"I see you pose as musicians," he went on, nodding at

101

the violin cases piled near the side wall of the tent. "I do not imagine that is your profession."

"Musicians we don't pose as, Cap," Sam said and this time he did not smile. His face was hard and ruthless as he leaned back tilting his chair and reached the near case. "I guess you better wise up your boys. Now don't jump and yell for help, Cap. All I'm going to do is show something to you." He unlatched the lid and lifted it.

Despite Sam's warning, Dietrich was startled. A submachine gun and a dozen clips of ammunition were in the case. Sam snapped the case shut and carelessly pushed it across the sand floor toward the wall. Of course, Dietrich remembered, shutting his eyes, that was the way American gangsters carried weapons about the city streets. He felt a passing wave of nausea. At any time during the last hour, these men could have murdered him and been out of the camp in their powerful car before anyone was aware of what had happened. Whatever business the Enna brothers had with him, he was convinced of their good intentions, but at the same time that he acknowledged a genuine feeling of fellowship with them, he burned with rage at Doeppler for failing to take elementary precautions.

"I won't mince words, Cap," Sam said, coldly serious now. "We're mobsters. You want a heist, snatch, somebody liquidated, that's our business. Like I said, it got too hot for us in the Windy City. We beat it. Now we got a little racket going in Tunis. Black Market stuff. Run in the contraband from Spain and Portugal, sh'p it out to the U.S.A., England, Germany, Italy. You want to check us out, that's okay. Get on the radio and have your boys in Tunis get out their files on the *Mercato Succoso Trading Corp.*, that's us. We do business with your boys, the top brass. We come here to help you, Cap."

"That's very thoughtful," Dietrich said with a smile. "You already have helped me to remember one of the pleasures life can hold."

"I guess we won't be forgetting this night either, Cap," Mark Enna said pleasantly, although he was scowling fiercely. Dietrich decided it must be a habit with these men to look ferocious.

"What did you have in mind we could work out together?" Dietrich asked, suspecting the Ennas wanted his

102

assistance in some Black Market operation.

"I know you ain't going to like this, Cap, but I got to tell you so you see why we're here," Sam said. "Cap, they're laughing at you in Tunis. At your headquarters and in the officer's clubs, at the bars and the casinos. They talk about a Rat Patrol and somebody says 'Dietrich' and you get a horse laugh. Everybody says this Rat Patrol has made a monkey out of you."

The blood drained from Dietrich's cheeks and he felt pale and frozen inside. "What do you know about the Rat Patrol?" he asked guardedly.

"Just what we hear, Cap," Sam said. "Common gossip, nothing official. They say this Rat Patrol are four GI commandos who tear around in jeeps blowing up your gas and ammunition. There's lots of stories about them. One is they took you prisoner and tied you up like a pig on a stick. Another is they came on you when you was taking a bath, stole all your clothes and you had to walk back to camp from the pool stark naked. They're saying it'd be better if you let yourself get shot by them instead of them always laughing at you like you didn't count."

"These stories about the Rat Patrol and me are prevalent throughout Tunis?" Dietrich asked in a lathering rage.

"Yeah, with your Army," Sam said. "I don't guess the Ay-rabs give a damn. You just take it easy, Cap. Getting mad ain't going to undo the dirt. You got to turn the trick. That's what we came to see you about. We got a proposition. We take the Rat Patrol on for you, rub them out nab them, whatever you say. The job has got a price tag. It's business with us, see? What do you say, Cap?"

"I think you are gracious men whose company I enjoy," Dietrich said evenly although inside he was smoldering at what Sam had told him. "I am afraid I must also tell you I think you are foolish. You have made a long and tiresome journey for nothing. We are two Armies opposing one another in the field. This Rat Patrol is comprised of soldiers. This is a military affair. What in heaven gave you the idea that four civilians inexperienced in war could succeed where a company of elite soldiers has failed?"

"From what we hear about the way they operate, these guys in the Rat Patrol ain't soldiers," Sam said. "They're

103

hoods just like us. They operate like us. Make a hit and run. They think like us. Do the job sneaky and dirty. Look, Cap, we're specialists in the rub-out. Like you said, we ain't soldiers and that's a plus. That Rat Patrol ain't going to tie a can on our tails if they spot us like they would your men. We can get next to them where you can't. We can get the job done."

"You're U.S. citizens; they are American soldiers," Dietrich pointed out. "Why would you be willing to kill them for an enemy of your country?"

"You forget, we got no country, Cap," Sam said. "We go back now, we get the hot seat. We already took our share of U.S. citizens for a ride. We do it for you for a fast buck. In Chicago the boys paid us five grand per head. We ain't going to stick you like that because maybe you ain't got that kind of dough and also, there's four of them. One grand each, four grand for the lot. Gun them down or grab them, you name it. What do you say, Cap?"

Dietrich's narrowed eyes wandered from one face to another. He thought he never in his life had seen such utterly dead eyes. None of them was smiling and in the harsh set of their features was death. There was no doubt of it. These men were killers. Indian lore was Dietrich's hobby and the name for such men burned in his mind. They were bounty hunters. He looked covertly at the violin cases and suddenly was very happy that they had not approached the American Colonel Wilson first and asked him to place a price on the Dietrich head.

Grosse stepped just inside the tent and his eyes jumped from Sam's to Jack's to Sol's to Mark's head. He looked at Dietrich, eyes flashing a warning as he shook his head violently.

"What is it, Grosse?" Dietrich snapped irritably.

"Is there anything else, sir?" he asked, continuing to shake his head negatively and pointing at the backs of the Enna brothers.

"That is all," Dietrich said angrily. "I'll call if I want you."

Grosse shook his head again and stepped out into the white light that continued to glare overhead from the flares.

"Very well," Dietrich said. "It is, as you call it, a deal. Shall we shake on it?"

104

Ceremoniously, each Enna brother stood to clasp Dietrich's hand.

"Now," Dietrich said, abruptly down to business. "I shall assist you as much as I am able. Until approximately nineteen hours, that is until seven o'clock last night, the Rat Patrol was in the American camp which lies in the desert valley below. Sometime soon after that, they departed in their two jeeps to the south. We had a patrol within the Allied lines which has not reported for almost twelve hours. I suspect that patrol is a victim of the Rat Patrol. The next report we have of them placed them on a ridge of land between two salt marshes traveling west. This was at a location approximately fifty miles south from here. We were testing robot mines at the area. The Rat Patrol destroyed the mines. The next clue we have is another patrol about fifty miles west and forty miles south which the Rat Patrol blew up killing four men. We have had patrols in halftracks out all day searching for the Rat Patrol, but there has been no further report of them."

"Looks like they was swinging wide to get at you from the rear, Cap," Sam said with a dark scowl. "They might be in your camp right now."

"That is possible," Dietrich admitted.

"If they was here, what would they be doing?" Sam asked. "Blowing up your gas and ammunition like they said in Tunis?"

"I think more likely they would be determining the location of the guns we have defending the ridge," Dietrich said. "They have a long range gun in the Allied area, a British twenty-five-pounder. If they could place the positions of my armor and guns, they could knock them out."

"They got a gun that can reach you?" Sam asked, apparently impressed with Dietrich's knowledge. "How'd you know that? Oh, I get it. You can see down in the valley from up here."

"Yes," Dietrich said. "But this gun is concealed. They have a pit where the Rat Patrol has kept the jeeps and where the four men have been living. That has been a deception. The pit contains the gun. I bought the information from some Arabs."

"You wasn't born yesterday, Cap," Sam said admiringly. "So we better start right here in your camp and work

105

through the gun positions. You want to give us the layout, Cap?"

"On top of the ridge, the heavy guns, 75 mm. cannon and rocket-launchers," Dietrich said unhesitatingly. "Down the slope, mortars and below them, machine guns and riflemen. At the bottom the field is mined, as well as trails and approaches on the slope."

"Sounds like you got yourself a fort, Cap," Sam said. "Okay, here's what we'll do. Two of us will work the ridge, the other two will slip down to them mortars. If we don't find anybody, then your Enna-buddies—" He stopped and laughed delightedly at his pun. His gold tooth gleamed. "Anyway, we'll go through the camp with a fine tooth comb. If we still don't find them, we'll move on outside the camp and do some slow driving in and out, enough to make them curious."

"Very well," Dietrich said with a smile. He had planned much the same operation himself within the camp and it pleased him that the professional killers suggested the same plan. He handed each of the Ennas his passport as he stood.

"We'll get started, Cap," Sam said. "Better pass the word. I'd hate to have some trigger-happy jerk mistake us for the Rat Patrol."

"I'll do that," Dietrich said with a laugh, "but I don't think anyone who has seen the Rat Patrol would make that mistake."

The Enna brothers had just filed out when Grosse darted into the tent.

"*Mein Hauptmann,* please," he said agitatedly. "You are making a mistake."

14

Troy walked rapidly toward the Hispano-Suiza that loomed in the fitfully lighted night some fifty yards west of Dietrich's tent. He heard Moffitt, Hitch and Tully scuffing at his heels. Two Mark IV tanks which had not been there before were parked behind the car. They seemed rather close together and blocked the way the car had come. He heard the slap of running feet and turned in time to see Dietrich's orderly, Grosse, outlined in profile before he dived inside the tent. The man disturbed him profoundly. His curiosity had been out of proportion and there was something uncertainly familiar about him that nagged at the back of Troy's mind.

"Dietrich's orderly is suspicious of us," Troy muttered under his voice as the others shouldered around him at the car. "Be ready to jump in and make a run for it. Sol, can you turn around with those tanks behind us?"

Tully looked to either side and considered the Mark IVs directly behind the car. "I'll back out, Sam," he said. "I'll squeeze between them."

"What makes that guy suspicious?" Hitch asked quietly, removing his tommy gun from the violin case. "We've never run into him before that I remember."

"We sold Dietrich sure as shooting," Tully said softly, edging toward the driver's side.

"Okay, boys," Troy said loudly, removing his submachine gun and slipping two clips of cartridges into his pocket. He tossed the case onto the back seat. "You know what to do. Sol, Mark, work the mortars from that grade to the ends and back. Jack and I will do likewise here on top."

A barrage of high explosive shells based somewhere down below and dust that flamed in redly burning clouds leapt above the ridge. Rocket launchers panted heavily and a cluster of magnesium flares trailing white smoke lighted the dark sky garishly. All along the ridge and slope, guns slammed shells down into the valley. Heavy firing crashed the floor of the desert. Dietrich broke from his tent at a dead run. Grosse stood in the entrance calling after him, *"Mein Hauptmann, mein Hauptmann, bitte."* Dietrich did not turn nor even hesitate.

"Think we ought to take care of Grosse?" Hitch murmured.

"Not now," Troy said. "We convinced Dietrich and Grosse didn't get a chance to sell whatever he's peddling. This attack gives us a break. Let's get this job done fast and get out while they've got their hands full. Use the grade as your reference. Remember what the weapons are and the paces between the emplacements. Now let's shake it."

Tully and Hitch trotted ahead and Moffitt and Troy jogged only slightly behind. Without further conversation Tully and Hitch plunged down the grade. Moffitt and Troy turned their backs to each other and started walking. Dust obscured the flare-lighted night as Troy paced off ten yards to a gun position. The weapon was a long-barreled Guerlich antitank gun that commanded the north side of the grade. The Guerlich was an odd weapon. It had a tapered barrel that reduced 28mm. shells ringed with soft iron bands to 20 mm. at the reinforced muzzle that looked like a funnel stuck into the barrel. The pressure built up within the barrel by gastight skirts slammed the shells out at forty-four hundred feet per second. There would be a similar weapon on Moffitt's side of the grade, Troy reasoned. A two-man crew manned the gun but it was not firing. The Jerries watched Troy curiously as he walked by with his submachine gun but they did not challenge him. He wondered whether Dietrich already had sent out word about the Enna brothers or if the men just didn't care.

The Shermans apparently were not firing at the ridge. Although Troy could not see where the shells were landing, he guessed Wilson was blasting the minefield. He wondered whether there could be any truth in the Arab's report to Dietrich that a British twenty-five-pounder now occupied

108

he pit where the jeeps had been stabled. It was possible Wilson had managed to get one in. It would explain the mission and the CO's refusal to disclose his reason for wanting the gun position. Well, the Arab had fixed that. If Wilson actually were working to clear a path through the minefield now, that meant a full-scaled attack on the ridge was imminent. Troy did not understand this. They were not expected to return with their information tonight, although, with luck, they might be able to return before dawn. They would not have the pattern of the minefield but apparently Wilson wasn't waiting for it. Except for Grosse, who hadn't hurt them yet, everything had fallen into place perfectly. If they could get the positions of the weapons while Dietrich was preoccupied with the shelling, they stood a good chance of getting out safely.

Ten paces from the antitank gun to an emplaced 75 mm. cannon. The weapon was banging away and the crew, brawny-shouldered and bare to the waist, did not look at him as he strode behind them. Ten paces to a rocket launcher, ten paces to another emplaced 75. Back off the ridge on either side of the rocket launcher were halftracks, maneuvering to turn around. Apparently Dietrich feared Wilson would use the twenty-five-pounder and was sending the halftracks back to the column of Mark IVs Troy had noticed at the western perimeter as they had driven in. There had been twenty-four of them and it had looked as if others were concealed under nets.

The positioning of the guns was consistent, a dug-in 75 every twenty yards starting with the first twenty yards from the grade. A rocket launcher every twenty yards starting with the first twenty yards from the antitank gun. He had counted four cannon when he saw Dietrich standing on a flat stone behind the next position, rigidly intent on the shelling. Troy slunk past him like a shadow. He did not think Dietrich noticed him.

Troy's side of the grade was fortified for two hundred yards with ten 75s and nine rocket launchers. Beyond the tenth cannon, the ridge became spired and was insurmountable. Troy swung around and started back. He had not been stopped nor questioned.

The shelling continued unabated from both sides. Wilson seemed to be having some success blowing mines, but

109

nothing indicated the Jerries were scoring hits in the swirling dust. But the din was terrible. The incessant hammering sounded like mighty sledges pounding on great hollow steel drums and each blow sent up another gritty gray billow which the flares and exploding shells ignited weirdly.

There was a half measure of truth in the information Dietrich had received about the Rat Patrol, Troy thought as he slithered past the Jerry commander again. Some men in the camp had been wearing Rat Patrol hats and caps, at least until nineteen hundred the night before, Troy thought with a stiff-lipped smile. It must have been the same Arab who'd disclosed the twenty-five-pounder who'd reported that the Rat Patrol had been around. Dietrich had been able to more or less pinpoint their route by the patrols they'd destroyed and the doodlebugs that had blown themselves up. He wondered how anyone who'd seen them could possibly have transformed the Hispano-Suiza touring car into two jeeps. That had been gratuitous assistance in the deception. The disguises had fooled everyone except Grosse. It irritated Troy that he could not place the man.

Suddenly he remembered. Grosse had been the driver for the Jerry colonel they had captured in the battle for Sidi Beda months before. Troy had thought they had knocked him out when they had dragged him from the staff car they stole and dumped him in Dietrich's tent. The man must have been conscious and had a chance to observe them. But what could he possibly have remembered from those brief moments months earlier that enabled him to identify them tonight?

Troy had his positions fixed and hurried away from the ridge and Dietrich, the shelling and the illuminated cloud of pulverized earth. When he passed Dietrich's tent, well off from the entrance, he glimpsed Grosse sitting on Dietrich's cot in the light of the lantern. The man's head was down and his hands were clasped on his knees. He was waiting for Dietrich to return.

Troy lighted a cigarette when he reached the car. In a few minutes, Moffitt came up.

"We've got to get out of here fast, Jack," Troy said. "Grosse was driver for that Jerry we nabbed at Sidi Beda and took to Sidi Abd. I'm positive he's recognized us, but can't figure out how he's done it. We fooled Dietrich, who knows us pretty well, and this bird only had a glimpse of us."

"Oh?" Moffitt was mildly surprised. "It's odd he should see something Dietrich didn't. Hard luck. Everything was going swimmingly." He chuckled. "You played your part well, Sam."

"I wish Sol and Mark would shake it," Troy grated. "We've got what we came for. Wilson's blasting a path through the minefield, so we can forget that." He stopped short. "You don't suppose he's coming right up without waiting for our information? That we got our heads shaved for nothing?"

"Look at it this way, Sam," Moffitt said, and in the flare light the J. Enna smile was a leer. "We've exchanged our hair for a ham and cheese sandwich."

There was a lull in the firing and Troy held his breath, searching toward the ridge for Tully and Hitch. He wondered what was delaying them. Then the guns bammed away again. Another lull. Half a dozen flares parachuted into shrouded night. The firing from the Shermans had fallen off to an intermittent shell or two. The Jerry guns hurled another dozen rounds. Machine gun and rifle fire still rapped from the slope. Perhaps there were sappers in the minefield. Abruptly all the heavy weapons were silent. Rifles still pinged. Troy thought he heard the clanking tracks of turning tanks.

Dietrich walked briskly back from the ridge and entered his tent. Still Hitch and Tully did not appear.

"Get in behind the wheel, Jack," Troy said tensely and flipped his gun off safety. "If anyone starts toward us, take off. I'll cover."

"I can't run off and leave the three of you behind," Moffitt protested.

"You're not exactly getting the frosting," Troy said and laughed shortly. "They'll be after you. At least you can tell Wilson what's on the ridge if you get through. On my side, every twenty yards starting from the grade, there was a 75 in place. Ten yards off the grade, a Guerlich AT. Every twenty yards from the Guerlich, a rocket launcher. Ten 75s. Nine launchers."

111

"The methodical Jerries followed the same pattern on the south side," Moffitt said.

The lieutenant, Doeppler, who had reported that he'd captured them, dragged a cursing, struggling Arab into Dietrich's tent.

"The officer of the guard has granted us a reprieve," Troy said and breathed heavily. "Whatever Grosse was telling Dietrich, he will question the Arab. He has as little business here as the Rat Patrol."

"Whatever can be keeping our boys?" Moffitt wondered aloud. "We've had a bit of luck so far. Perhaps Wilson has a way cleared and will provide more diversionary action."

"We can hope," Troy said, lighting another cigarette. "I'm not going to feel like cheering until we're on our way."

Grosse stepped from the tent. He turned his head toward the car and looked at them for a moment, then walked quickly toward the ridge. Tully and Hitch trotted up the grade and ran past him. He turned and watched but made no attempt to stop them.

"Get ready," Troy said, adding quickly as he heard the ignition switch click, "not yet. Don't call attention until the last minute."

Doeppler came out of the tent, saw Hitch and Tully, held up his hand, stopped them and motioned them inside the tent.

"Get moving, Jack," Troy snarled, bringing his tommy gun around at his hip. No starter whirred. The only sound that came from the car was the shuffling of feet.

"Can't find the activator," Moffitt said quietly.

"Up by the clutch pedal, on the floor," Troy hissed in exasperation. Doeppler was walking toward him.

"Can't locate it, old boy," Moffitt said and Troy knew that he was deliberately stalling. Doeppler had almost reached him and Troy dropped his tommy gun. The lieutenant touched his arm and pointed toward the tent with his machine pistol. Troy swore under his breath and started walking.

"Wait a bit," Moffitt called. "I'll be along with you."

15

Corporals Merriam and Heath with Privates Albright and Kierzek had reported to Wilson as directed at nineteen hundred. Albright and Kierzek, who had impersonated Hitch and Tully, were meek by comparison with the corporals. They were slack-jawed boys with worried eyes and not much character development showing in their smooth-cheeked faces. Each of them was wearing a helmet and field jacket and carrying a tommy gun. Wilson sent Peilowski for the Arab who had been detained under guard in a supply truck. He had been provided with rations and a blanket and had spent most of the day sleeping.

"The Arab informs me it is approximately five miles to the trail," Wilson said, thinking the men looked ill in the greenish light from the lantern on his table. Maybe they did feel sick. It was not a usual patrol. He felt a little sorry for Albright and Kierzek. "You will depart this camp at nineteen-thirty. When the enemy fires his usual flares, you will go to the ground and remain motionless if the area in which you are traveling is illuminated. Without resorting to force, you will see that the Arab does not attract attention to you."

"How we going to do that, say 'please'?" Merriam growled.

"Merriam," Wilson said severely and his eyes were icy. "If you think you will be replaced on this mission because you are insubordinate, you are wrong. I shall, however, prefer charges against you when you return unless the assignment is carried out exactly as I order. Do you understand?"

"Yes, sir," Merriam said sullenly.

"I am allowing one and one-half hours for you to reach the trail. At twenty-one hundred, you will begin the ascent and the Arab will start back. At that hour, tanks will commence diversionary fire on the north side of the grade. When you reach the ridge, penetrate the Jerry perimeter if possible. I do not want you to risk revealing yourselves because I plan to use this trail again, but I do want you to determine as well as you can the type and location of the enemy weapons at the southern end of the ridge. This information is particularly vital at this immediate time and I shall be personally grateful if you return with it. Is this clear?"

"Yes, sir," Heath said, for the first time showing interest.

"Observe the Arab closely at all times," Wilson continued. "I do not believe this is a trick. If it is, I believe I can outbid the Jerries." He pointed at a canvas bag on the table. "That is your insurance. If the Arab does anything untoward or there is indication of deception, return with him at once. Under no circumstances mistreat him. Restrain him if you must but do not injure him."

"Yes, sir," Merriam said without enthusiasm.

The Arab came into the tent like a cat, silent and wary. Peilowski followed. His face was flushed and sweaty and he was puffing.

"Anything wrong?" Wilson asked quickly.

Peilowski shook his head. "Nothing wrong," he said. "He just moves faster than I do."

Wilson smiled fleetingly and spoke to the Arab. "Show the men the trail." He lifted the canvas bag and let it fall. It thunked solidly. He opened it and took out a handful of silver. "More than one hundred dollars," he said impressively. "A great deal more. You will be well rewarded. When you have shown my men the trail, return to my tent at once. You will be made comfortable. When my men have returned safely, the money will be given to you and you may leave."

Wilson thought Merriam looked relieved.

"Effendi," the Arab wailed. "I show the trail. How can I be sure they will be safe? Danger always awaits the man who enters the camp of his enemy. When I point the trail, I

114

have done what I say I do. You pay me."

"I am not asking you to guarantee against the normal perils of war," Wilson said. "If they meet with an accident and it is not a trap, you still will be paid for showing them the trail. I will know if there has been deceit. I must safeguard my men. You will be paid when they return or when it is shown that you have acted in good faith with us."

"Last night we use the trail," the Arab argued. "Then it is safe. It is all I guarantee."

"Let us take him with us to the top," Merriam suggested. "He can go first, lead the way."

"No," Wilson said. "If there is a trap, he would only lead you directly into it. I believe the Jerries mistreated him and his companions and he is telling the truth. Don't forget the attraction of the money." He lifted the bag and dropped it again, reminding the Arab, "A great deal more than one hundred dollars if you carry out your part of the bargain."

The Arab's eyes burned greedily. "I carry the bargain."

Wilson looked at his watch. "It is nearly nineteen-thirty," he said. "Good luck, Merriam, Heath, Albright, Kierzek. I'll be waiting here for you, whatever the hour."

About twenty-hundred, Jerry rockets began firing the usual parachute flares over the valley. Wilson left the tent, walking between the halftracks to the lead Sherman in the V of tanks. He watched the globes of bright light as they floated over the desert. It was a gay and spectacular sight, but tonight he wished he could dispense with it. While he had no intention of sending his armor within effective range of the ridge, he did want the first shells to come as a surprise and jar the Jerries. The flares tonight came in clusters and in no pattern. There would be a group to the north, a group to the south, a second and third group to the south and then the northern edge of the field would light up. Abruptly there was darkness, then flares flashed all along the line and died away. The desert was dark again.

At twenty-thirty, during an interlude when no flares hung in the sky, Wilson ordered out the lead tank and the three tanks flanking it. The hulking M4s ground across the desert, their engines pounding, each pulling thirty-six tons of welded steel plate and armament ahead at a cautious ten miles per hour, less than half their top speed. The V closed

115

quickly as the tanks drove for a position to the right of the grade. As they neared the minefield which extended into the desert from the foot of the slope, the tanks maneuvered, aligning in a staggered diagonal file. The 75s opened fire, smashing at the sand in a carefully directed path that reached toward the grade. The shells shrieked, a few mines blew and sand geysers spouted into the air.

Rockets showered the sky with flares and for a moment before roiled sand spume hid them, the tanks stood stark behind fire-spouting gun barrels on the desert. The hill flashed and puffed and roared as cannon, rockets, mortars and even machine guns and rifles began to fire in a frenzied outburst. The hill erupted like a volcano spewing fiery lava. The night shook.

Wilson stood in his staff car parked half a mile behind the last tank. He had left Peilowski at HQ with the canvas bag of silver and had asked Corporal Locke to drive him and get a change of scenery. Locke was enjoying the show. He craned so intently, Wilson knew his neck would be stiff in the morning. Wilson removed his glasses and handed them to Locke. Actually they were worthless and the result of the firing on the minefield was difficult to assess because of the dust storm that raged under the pounding shells. Now and again he heard the muffled blast of an exploding mine, but there weren't enough of them to satisfy him. He smiled a little grimly and reminded himself that this was not a serious effort and would do little good other than to occupy the Jerries while Merriam and his small squad crept up the secret trail. Jerry would be down to lay new mines when the tanks pulled back.

He gave a good show for one hour and at twenty-two-hundred ordered the tanks to withdraw. It should have been ample time for Merriam to get to the top, he thought as Locke whisked him back to his tent. He half expected the Arab to be waiting for him when he stepped into HQ but the native had not returned. Peilowski was stabbing at his typewriter and Wilson told him to knock off for the night.

"Build a fire, see if you can get some water to boil. Let's have hot coffee for a change," he said.

"Yes, sir," Peilowski agreed. He gathered paper and two

116

waxed ration containers from the tin can he used as a wastebasket. He half filled a half-gallon peach can and carried the paper and can outside the tent. He scooped a hole in the sand, and when a small fire blazed, he placed the can over it and went back into the tent for canteen cups and powdered coffee. Sitting beside the fire, he fed it continuously with bits of the waxed cardboard.

Wilson went out, glancing at the moonlighted, starry blue velvet sky that still was streaked with the smoke and dust of battle. He sat on the other side of the fire from Peilowski, gave him a cigarette and lighted one for himself. For a few moments they smoked without speaking.

"A C-47 will touch down at ten-hundred in the morning," Wilson finally said casually.

"Oh, yes, the one we've prepared the runway for," Peilowski said as if he'd known all about it all the time.

Wilson hid his smile. "We shall have a guest—overnight at least. Do you think you could find another cot somewhere around the camp?" Although Wilson had never mentioned it, he knew that Peilowski had a cot he used himself in the back of a supply truck he'd preempted.

Peilowski hesitated. Wilson knew it wasn't so much giving up the cot for a night as admitting its existence that bothered him. "I've always had the greatest respect for a first sergeant's ability to provide the impossible under the most difficult circumstances," Wilson said with a straight face. "The cot would of course be returned promptly to its rightful owner and no questions asked."

"Yes, sir," Peilowski said. "I'll try to manage something."

"And can you rustle up something a little different in the way of rations?" Wilson asked. "Are there any five-in-one rations with meat stew and canned fruit?"

"I guess I can dig up something in the way of chow," Peilowski said, but this time he scowled. "Seems to me it ought to be the other way around. Somebody coming into a combat area from the outside ought to bring us something decent to eat."

Wilson laughed. "I agree but I'm afraid we're out of luck. This man is coming from the States, where civilians are issued food stamps and have the idea they're rationed

117

so we can have steaks and butter three times a day. If h should bring any food, you can prepare it and take you share."

The water never came to a boil, but it was hotter tha usual and they drank their coffee outside. After Peilowsl had kicked sand over the cardboard embers, they wer back into the tent. Twenty-two-thirty crawled by and twen ty-three-hundred. The Arab still did not return. Wilso stared at the bag of money and worried. Nothing short c death could have prevented the Arab from laying claim t his reward. Wilson smoked nervously. He became increas ingly more certain that some disaster had overtaken Mer riam's squad and the Arab.

At twenty-three-thirty, Albright and Kierzek stumble into HQ. They were babbling incoherently and their eye were dull with shock. Kierzek's face was pinched with pai and one side was covered from temple to chin with cor gealed blood. Albright's left leg dragged.

"What happened?" Wilson exclaimed, jumping from h' chair and helping first Albright and then Kierzek to hi cot. "Peilowski, get a medic. Where are Merriam an Heath? And the Arab?"

"The Arab . . . came back?" Albright gasped an winced.

"No," Wilson said, and added softly, "tell me what hap pened."

"If he . . . didn't come back . . . then it was a trap," Al bright managed with great difficulty.

Peilowski rushed from the tent.

"The trap," Wilson urged quietly.

"Kierzek and me . . . we thought so . . . he'd of con back . . . if he didn't know."

"Know what?" Wilson said gently.

"The trail he showed us," Kierzek answered. He glance at the bloodied left pants leg of his fatigues and gritted h teeth. "It hurts," he said. "It kept going out under me and had to crawl."

"I've sent for a medic," Wilson said comfortingly, a though he knew it was small comfort to a man in pain. F lighted two cigarettes, gave one to Kierzek and placed tl other between Albright's lips. "Can you tell me about tl trail?"

118

"It was mined," Kierzek said and gritted his teeth again. "He showed it to us and beat it. There was horse droppings on it. Merriam decided the Arab had told the truth. About using it. We started up. Merriam first. Then Heath. We were maybe ten, maybe fifteen, feet behind. Merriam must of stepped over a Shu mine, because when he got it up ahead, Heath behind him went up in pieces too. Damn pieces of both of them flying all over. I got smacked in the face with something sticky. It was worse than the shrapnel. Damn Arab didn't come back for his money. He knew it was mined and beat it."

16

Dietrich had hurried back to his tent as soon as the Allied shelling had stopped. He still did not know quite what to make of the rather foolish attack on the minefield. At first he had feared Wilson would open with the twenty-five-pounder and his column would roar through the path the line of tanks had cleared. After an hour, however, the Shermans had withdrawn. He had sent a squad of sappers to patch up the field. Rockets still were firing flares but the dust was settling.

Grosse was waiting for him, sitting on the edge of the cot as if it belonged to him. Dietrich was furious with Grosse. He did not understand the man's boorish attitude this evening. He had been vexing whenever he was in the tent. Grosse had been trying to babble something when the first shells exploded. Now he jumped to his feet as Dietrich stepped into the tent. Dietrich brushed past him without a word and poured himself a glass of brandy.

"Herr Hauptmann," Grosse said nervously, timidly ap-

proaching the table. "All evening I have tried to warn you. I hope it is not too late. The men who are here calling themselves the Enna brothers. They are the Rat Patrol."

"Grosse, have you been at the brandy?" Dietrich asked in utter disbelief. "The Enna brothers are exactly what they admit themselves to be. They are American gangsters. You forget I am well acquainted with the Rat Patrol. You think because they are American and there are the four of them, that they are the Rat Patrol. They are not. For your information, they are looking for the Rat Patrol to kill them."

"I am sorry, *mein Hauptmann*," Grosse said stubbornly although he paled. "Those men are the Rat Patrol. They have disguised themselves."

"Grosse, you have always discharged your duties with competence, but now I think you are more than somewhat mad," Dietrich said. "Troy, Moffitt, Hitch and Tully have eyes of various colors, none of which I recall to be dark brown. Also their hair runs from light to dark, but I do not think anyone of them has black hair and I believe the hair of one to be bright red. No one of the Rat Patrol possesses a gold tooth. No one of the Rat Patrol whom I observed as recently as yesterday had grown a mustache. I have talked with each of the Rat Patrol on many occasions. Pettigrew has a slow way of speaking that, I believe, is from the southern states. Moffitt has a decided Etonian or Oxford accent. Troy comes from the midwest, I think, and Hitch has certain mannerisms in his speech that suggest the east. Each of the Sicilian-Americans who were here tonight speaks the same cant or argot that in motion pictures at least is associated with what the Americans call mobsters. The men are killers, yes. They were alone in the tent with me and each had a machine gun in the violin case he carried. Can you imagine what the Rat Patrol would have done with me under such circumstances? Please, Grosse, leave me alone and do not bother me again tonight."

"I regret, *mein Hauptmann*," Grosse said miserably, "I still must insist they are the Rat Patrol. You forget, I also am acquainted with them. They overpowered me at Sidi Beda. I studied each carefully so I would recognize him if we ever should encounter one another again. I was an art student before I entered military service. An artist must study anatomy, bone structure as well as physiognomy. They told me I was particularly gifted at the structure, particularly of heads and I planned to be a portrait artist. Forget the color of the hair and eyes, remove the mustaches, view these men in profile, and you will recognize the Rat Patrol."

Irritated as he was, Dietrich considered it. He wished he had not returned the passports, although the pictures in them were full face. He tried to recall Sam, the one he remembered best, but the only image he could focus in his mind was a fiercely smiling face, a gold tooth and hard dark eyes. He simply could not make Sam Enna come out as Troy or Moffitt—or either of the two privates, for that matter.

"Grosse," he said, "I accept that your concern is real, but your fantastic suspicions are entirely unfounded. On one point alone, you are defeated. I have pointed out to you the color of the Enna brothers' eyes is dark brown."

"There are ways of changing the color of eyes," Grosse said.

"Oh, come now," Dietrich said, out of patience. "A field commander scarcely goes into battle equipped with colored contact lenses. And do not tell me those black heads of hair are wigs. Such disguises call for elaborate preparations which are not available to someone in the field."

"The Rat Patrol could have been flown to Cairo in that bomber," Grosse persisted.

"I told you I myself saw them in their camp yesterday," Dietrich snapped, losing his temper. "As late as last evening, they were in their camp. Their movements from the time they left the camp in their jeeps are known. You have allowed the Rat Patrol to become your personal bogey man. I will have no more of this nonsense."

"*Herr Hauptmann* Dietrich," Grosse said stiffly. "Will you bring the men into your tent and permit me to examine them?"

"No!" Dietrich shouted. "I will not subject them to such an indignity."

Doeppler interrupted. He dragged a screeching Arab into the tent.

"Now what is it?" Dietrich said, beginning to shake with rage.

"One of those sneaking Arabs who was here last night," Doeppler said. "I caught him stealing into ca᎐p again."

"And so you have taken yet another prisoner, Doeppler," Dietrich said with deadly calm and then he exploded. "You idiot. I invited Haffi to come back whenever he had information. Remove your hands from him." He turned to the Arab. "I am sorry, Haffi. It has been an unfortunate mistake." He stood and carried his canvas chair around the table. "Please be seated. I shall sit upon the cot. You returned because you have something to tell me?"

"You have had no reason to complain," Haffi said resentfully, glaring at Doeppler.

"Your information has a certain value," Dietrich said. "They have not used the gun yet, but I think they are preparing to. We are removing our armor to safety. What new report do you carry?"

"You have not heard that certain men have been destroyed?" Haffi asked.

"What men?" Dietrich asked, puzzled.

"So you have not learned of it," Haffi said with satisfaction. "I am pleased that I can tell you and of the part I took. You will pay, of course, according to the value."

"That is understood," Dietrich said gravely.

"I tricked them into destroying themselves," Haffi said gleefully. At the moment he did not look at all Arabian. "You spoke of the Rat Patrol last night. The men who wear the peculiar hats. The one in the hat that seems more civilian than military injured my arm so severely I fear I shall never use it again. You can forget them. They are dead."

"The men of the Rat Patrol are dead!" Dietrich exclaimed, not yet believing the report but turning triumphantly to Grosse. He looked quickly back to the Arab. "Tell me the entire story."

"Last night I heard you order that the secret trail we had used to enter your camp be fortified with the explosives you bury in the ground," Haffi said. He indicated Doeppler. "When this officer returned later, he reported to you that the charges had been placed. Today I returned to the camp of your enemy. I arranged to be captured by the man of the Rat Patrol who wears the civilian hat, the same man who had beaten me before. Things performed themselves as I had planned and this man again twisted my arm and pained me."

"Just a minute," Dietrich said suspiciously. "At what hour was this?"

"Somewhat after the time the sun had passed its zenith," Haffi said.

It was possible, Dietrich thought. Doeppler had seen them at midnight. Soon after that they had blown up Stengle's patrol. They could even have been in and out of his camp and returned over the ridge between the salt marshes to their own lines before noon. None of the halftracks had discovered any trace of them.

"Go on," he told Haffi.

"They held me prisoner until it was dark," Haffi said bitterly. "Their commander told me he would pay me five hundred dollars in silver if I would show them the path my companions and I had used to reach your camp last night. I agreed to show it to this Rat Patrol and the four of them went with me. I took them to the trail, and when they saw that horses recently had been over it, they believed I spoke the truth and started to walk up it. I concealed myself and watched. The two who seemed to be the leaders—the one who wore the civilian hat and the one who wore a dark, soft flat cap without a visor—were in the lead, but tonight all were wearing helmets."

"Are you certain they were the same men?" Dietrich interrupted.

"Of course," Haffi said indignantly. "I do not forget a man who injures me. I expect a reward but also I wanted revenge."

"All were destroyed by the mines?" Dietrich asked, checking his mounting excitement.

"I know you hold that the truth is not always spoken by an Arab and I am sorry that often you are right," Haffi said earnestly. "I shall not deceive you in any way because all of what I can say you can discover for yourself. The two men who were in the front were all blown up in pieces. The other two, who seemed to be of lesser rank, were disabled, but they were not killed. They dragged themselves away. I did all of this at a great sacrifice to myself because I could not return and claim the five hundred silver dollars they offered me."

123

"If what you tell me is true, you shall n̶o̶
money," Dietrich said. "Doeppler, you ar̶e̶
guard. Have you had no report?"

"The shelling has just now stopped, Her̶
Doeppler said. "I must excuse the men guar̶
if they did not call in during the battle."

Dietrich pointed to the telephone on his
a field telephone with a connection near tha̶
perimeter. Use it."

Dietrich watched Grosse narrowly as Do̶
contact. Grosse appeared bewildered or
shame, Dietrich thought. The man had serv̶e̶
he would have to be replaced. If he had kn̶
been an art student, he never would have p̶
sensitive position he had occupied as dri̶
Artists often were unstable. He returned to̶

"The two men who were injured re̶t̶
camp?" Dietrich asked.

"I started after them with my knife but
it," Haffi said. "Although they seemed to
they still had their weapons."

"Since you knew the path was mined a̶
men killed on it, how did you get here this̶

"I climbed over the rocks like a goat
Dietrich the palms of his hands. Tough
they were, they had been ripped and we̶
dried blood.

Doeppler ended his telephone convers̶a̶
at Dietrich.

"The guard confirms the Arab's story
he reported. "A four-man patrol was obs̶e̶
There were two explosions almost simult̶a̶
first two men were actually blown apart a̶n̶
other two men appeared to be injured but
ger away. The guard has been unable to
because of the mines that are in place."

Haffi spoke excitedly. "You see, Capt̶
valuable information, I perform extensi̶v̶
speak the truth."

"You speak the truth and you will ha̶
Dietrich looked at Grosse. "You may lea̶
When Grosse had gone, Dietrich light̶e̶

124

had planned and this man again twisted my arm and pained me."

"Just a minute," Dietrich said suspiciously. "At what hour was this?"

"Somewhat after the time the sun had passed its zenith," Haffi said.

It was possible, Dietrich thought. Doeppler had seen them at midnight. Soon after that they had blown up Stengle's patrol. They could even have been in and out of his camp and returned over the ridge between the salt marshes to their own lines before noon. None of the halftracks had discovered any trace of them.

"Go on," he told Haffi.

"They held me prisoner until it was dark," Haffi said bitterly. "Their commander told me he would pay me five hundred dollars in silver if I would show them the path my companions and I had used to reach your camp last night. I agreed to show it to this Rat Patrol and the four of them went with me. I took them to the trail, and when they saw that horses recently had been over it, they believed I spoke the truth and started to walk up it. I concealed myself and watched. The two who seemed to be the leaders—the one who wore the civilian hat and the one who wore a dark, soft flat cap without a visor—were in the lead, but tonight all were wearing helmets."

"Are you certain they were the same men?" Dietrich interrupted.

"Of course," Haffi said indignantly. "I do not forget a man who injures me. I expect a reward but also I wanted revenge."

"All were destroyed by the mines?" Dietrich asked, checking his mounting excitement.

"I know you hold that the truth is not always spoken by an Arab and I am sorry that often you are right," Haffi said earnestly. "I shall not deceive you in any way because all of what I can say you can discover for yourself. The two men who were in the front were all blown up in pieces. The other two, who seemed to be of lesser rank, were disabled, but they were not killed. They dragged themselves away. I did all of this at a great sacrifice to myself because I could not return and claim the five hundred silver dollars they offered me."

"If what you tell me is true, you shall not suffer for the money," Dietrich said. "Doeppler, you are officer of the guard. Have you had no report?"

"The shelling has just now stopped, *Herr Hauptmann,*" Doeppler said. "I must excuse the men guarding that sector if they did not call in during the battle."

Dietrich pointed to the telephone on his table. "There is a field telephone with a connection near that position of the perimeter. Use it."

Dietrich watched Grosse narrowly as Doeppler made his contact. Grosse appeared bewildered or dazed. It was a shame, Dietrich thought. The man had served him well, but he would have to be replaced. If he had known Grosse had been an art student, he never would have placed him in the sensitive position he had occupied as driver and orderly. Artists often were unstable. He returned to Haffi.

"The two men who were injured returned to their camp?" Dietrich asked.

"I started after them with my knife but thought better of it," Haffi said. "Although they seemed to be severely hurt, they still had their weapons."

"Since you knew the path was mined and had seen two men killed on it, how did you get here this time?"

"I climbed over the rocks like a goat." Haffi showed Dietrich the palms of his hands. Tough and callused as they were, they had been ripped and were covered with dried blood.

Doeppler ended his te'_phone conversation and looked at Dietrich.

"The guard confirms the Arab's story in every detail," he reported. "A four-man patrol was observed on the trail. There were two explosions almost simultaneously and the first two men were actually blown apart and shattered. The other two men appeared to be injured but were able to stagger away. The guard has been unable to go down the path because of the mines that are in place."

Haffi spoke excitedly. "You see, Captain, I bring you valuable information, I perform extensive services, and I speak the truth."

"You speak the truth and you will have your reward." Dietrich looked at Grosse. "You may leave."

When Grosse had gone, Dietrich lighted a cigarette and

124

sat silently thoughtful for a long time. He was considering the deaths of Troy and Moffitt and the fate of Tully and Hitch, who still lived.

"Doeppler," he finally said. "Have you any idea where the Enna brothers are?"

"Two were by the motor car," Doeppler said. "The other two had not returned from the mortars."

"Find them and bring them in," Dietrich said reluctantly. He did not like the decision he just had made. To the Arab he said, "Haffi, if you will leave when these men come, please. We have some business to discuss for a short while and then I shall deal with you."

"Certainly, *effendi,*" Haffi said, standing with his hands clasped and bowing as he backed from the tent. "I will be outside next to your tent when you are ready."

Sol and Mark Enna stepped inside, turning to watch the Arab as he left.

"I think the looey meant we should come in," Sol said uncertainly. "That right, Cap?"

"Yes," Dietrich said, dusting off the chair on which Haffi had sat and replacing it behind his table. "We shall wait a moment for Sam and Jack."

Sam was shaking his head as he poked it into the tent. "Sorry, Cap, but I'm certain the Rat Patrol isn't in your camp." Jack came in and stood beside him. Each dangled his submachine gun and Dietrich wondered again at Grosse's complete stupidity.

"I also am satisfied they are not in the camp," he said. "The two leaders, Sergeants Troy and Moffitt, have just been killed. They, with the Privates Pettigrew and Hitchcock, were endeavoring to re-enter the camp over an Arab trail. I had been informed of the path and it had been mined. Troy and Moffitt stepped on mines and were blown up."

"The two big Rats were exterminated?" Sam said incredulously. "Hey, Cap, that hits us where it hurts."

"Yes, I can appreciate that," Dietrich said with a wry smile. "The two privates were injured but escaped back to their lines."

"I guess you wouldn't be interested in them mice, Cap," Sam said sorrowfully.

"That is where you are wrong, Sam," Dietrich said.

125

"Each member of this Rat Patrol was resourceful in his own way. As long as Hitchcock and Pettigrew are alive, it is possible a new Rat Patrol may be formed with them as the nucleus. I want you to eliminate them."

"Why, sure, Cap," Sam said with a pleased smile that displayed his flamboyant tooth. Dietrich wondered whether the capping had been necessary. He remembered African tribal chieftains he had seen who had embellished their teeth with diamonds. "Tell us how to get to them," Sam went on. "We'll take care of them. You said you had mined the bottom of the slope. Is there some way we can get around?"

"Yes," Dietrich said. "You can drive west for fifty miles, south for fifty miles through the desert, across a treacherous ridge that the Rat Patrol managed both ways with jeeps, but which I doubt you could cross with your car, then north fifty miles into their camp. Such a trip, if you were able to complete it, would require endless explanation to the American commander. Not only that, it would take a good deal of time. If the injuries suffered by Pettigrew and Hitchcock are serious, as I am certain they must be, they will be evacuated by aircraft in the morning. You must reach them tonight."

"There's a ocean up north a ways," Jack said. "We can take a boat."

"Again there is the time element," Dietrich said. "It would take too long to reach the ocean, too long to walk to the Allied camp if you did make a safe landing. There is, however, a direct and relatively fast approach to their camp. You see, when we lay a minefield, we leave a safe passage through it for our own use."

"That's cute, Cap," Sam said. "So we leave here and just drive into their camp over your safe way."

"It isn't quite that simple," Dietrich said with a smile. "Driving into their camp through a minefield would be most difficult to explain. I am afraid you shall have to walk. It will be a stroll of about five miles. It will be tiresome but it will be safe."

"I see what you mean, Cap," Sam said doubtfully. "You're going to send a guide with us?"

"For part of the distance," Dietrich said. "For your own

126

protection, I suggest you leave your machine guns behind. If you are discovered, they would do you little good and you would not want to risk using them on Hitchcock and Pettigrew. You would arouse the entire company. I shall give you knives and I have observed that you have a pistol, Sam, which I hope you will not need to use. I dislike mentioning such a grisly detail, but I shall require some proof that you have completed this job."

"Like their hearts?" Sam said mercilessly and grinned fiendishly. "I gotcha, Cap. Can do."

"Good, Sam," Dietrich said. "Now, I do not want you to misunderstand, but one of you will remain here. Not as a hostage but as a guest until the rest of you return."

Sam laughed heartily. "You're sharp, Cap. We told you all we care about is a fast buck. You figure we've had a look around, we might be tempted to sell out to the Americans. We couldn't do it, Cap. Before he'd talk to us, he'd be calling Washington and we'd be on our way to the hotseat. We got more to lose than you, Cap, if we get picked up."

"Do you object to my terms, Sam?" Dietrich asked.

"Absolutely not," Sam said emphatically. "I'll stay here myself. The boys can handle a simple job like this. You and me will have a time. I got a bottle of bourbon in my bag and there should be some more left in my flask. You play stud poker?"

Dietrich leaned back chuckling. "I would enjoy that, Sam, I honestly would," he said. "But I sense in you the inherent qualities of a leader and I'm sure that if difficulties should arise, you will find a way to talk yourself around them." He turned to Jack. "If you have no objections, Mr. Jack Enna, you will remain with me. I shall do my best to make you comfortable."

"Sure, Captain," Jack said. "Anything you say."

"You can dig the bourbon out of my bag, Jack," Sam said. "Don't let Cap get pie-eyed. We'll be back before sunup. You watch for us."

"We'll do that, Sam," Jack said.

Dietrich spoke briefly with Doeppler and the lieutenant left the tent. Dietrich spoke to all of them but looked at Sam. "Doeppler will bring knives and some men. Someone will be watching for you at the bottom of the slope to lead you back. Also, you will be led down. I hope you do not think what I must do is inhospitable. You will understand, I am sure, Sam. Each of you will be blindfolded until you reach the bottom."

17

After the Jerry lieutenant, Doeppler, had tightly blindfolded Hitch, Tully and Troy, he gave each of them a series of twirls. Troy smiled as he was spun to the left and to the right several times. He did not try to count the number of turns he made in each direction. It was ridiculous. There was only one way they could be led, east to go down the slope. The lieutenant snapped an order and someone seized Troy's arm. He heard the lieutenant step out ahead and order, *"Vorwärts."*

The hand tugged and Troy stepped forward counting steps from the front of Dietrich's tent. He already had the position of the tent with relation to the slope well fixed in his mind. He counted fifty paces straight ahead, or east. He was turned and walked twenty paces north, then east twenty paces, and another twenty paces to the north. Now thirty paces east, fifty south, thirty east and his feet stumbled as the path sloped down. He repeated the directions he had been led to impress them on his mind, adding and subtracting to figure their position. Even before his feet told him he was on a relatively smooth surface free from obstacles, he knew he was on the grade, ten paces north and a hundred and thirty paces east of Dietrich's tent. He was happy the Germans were a methodical nation. If he had been walked in circles and diagonals, it might have been difficult to ascertain his position so exactly. But in any event, he would have realized he was being led down the grade so it really didn't matter.

Methodical Jerry might be, but the simple logic in leaving the grade unmined as the safe passage amazed Troy. It was the obvious that confused. The Jerries had planted one mine at the beginning of the grade and Runstead's tank had struck it. Wilson, and everyone else, had assumed that the grade being the direct and easy route to the pass was heavily sown with explosives. If the one mine hadn't been detonated, sappers would have had an easy task removing it when Dietrich was ready to pull off the ridge. Troy no longer bothered to count. Occasionally he stumbled and grumbled about the roughness of the trail. Perhaps one of the guards understood English and it would be in character for city rats like the Enna brothers in pointed shoes to complain about the hardships of the trail.

Grosse had done his best to sell Dietrich his suspicions about the Enna brothers, but they'd been saved again by a lucky break. Who had been killed and who had identified the men as the Rat Patrol? The Arab? He'd seen the grubby little jackal lurking outside Dietrich's tent, free and unmolested after the lieutenant had dragged him in. Troy decided they probably had a score to settle with the man. But mostly he was bothered with Grosse. If he knew they were the Rat Patrol, where had they slipped up?

The first order of business was to get Moffitt off the ridge. They had what they'd come for, including the location of the safe passage. They hadn't been able to get the disposition of the machine guns and infantry, but their fire would be like hail pelting the armored column when it swarmed up the grade. What had been the purpose of Wilson's shelling? Had he really intended to blast a way through the devil's garden of mines? He still would have the direct fire from the mortars, rockets and 75s to meet and that would be deadly until he could pinpoint the locations of the weapons. What was going on? Did he really have a British twenty-five-pounder? It all was very confusing.

Troy felt his feet on level ground and for a time was led straight ahead. To the edge of the minefield, he concluded. Then the spinning ceremony was repeated and the pattern

129

of the walking went something like north, east, west, south and north, although he did not pay much attention to it and did not bother counting paces. He could find the grade. When the blindfold was removed, he saw they were standing in the open desert perhaps half a mile from the grade. Glancing about, he saw a squad already repairing the damage the tanks had done, laying new mines in the field. The night was not luminescent, but the moon was out and Troy felt starkly conspicuous. Perhaps they couldn't be seen through the dust haze from Wilson's camp three miles away but he wanted to be moving.

"Whew," he said, shaking his head. "I'm dizzy. How we going to find you guys when we come back? Anybody here speak English?"

The lieutenant, standing a few yards apart from his enlisted men and the three civilians, spoke sharply to the owl-eyed boy in glasses with the dumpling cheeks who'd guided Hitch and still clung to his arm. He puffed and said in good but grossly accented English, "The lieutenant said I should tell you that we shall wait somewhere back on the slope in one of our fortified positions. We will watch for you to approach and one of us will come down to meet you."

"Sure, okay," Troy said. He hadn't counted on this. It was unexpected and he didn't like it. He had assumed that Doeppler, since he was officer of the guard, would return to the ridge with his men and a time and place for rendezvous set for several hours later. He had planned to send Tully and Hitch on to HQ and slip back to Dietrich's tent immediately to release Moffitt. It complicated matters to have Doeppler and his three men watching.

He looked across the three miles of open desert and glanced at the sky. There were no clouds. "We can't go straight across," he said. "They would see us even if we crawled. Tell the lieutenant we are going to circle the camp to the south and go in from the other side, where they won't be watching so closely. Okay?"

"Okey dokey," owl face said and giggled, obviously proud of his Americanism.

"Also tell him this is going to take a while," Troy said. "I guess three hours at the least, so when you get settled you might as well get some sleep. Not all at once, one of you stay awake and keep watching for us. If we run into anything we might have to come back fast."

"I will repeat what you have said," the boy told Troy.

The lieutenant listened impassively and said, *"Alles in Ordnung."*

"Now he said 'Okey dokey,'" the boy said with another giggle.

"Okey dokey yourself, pal," Troy said. "We're off."

He ran straight south at a steady jog with Hitch and Tully at his heels. He maintained the pace for ten minutes before he stopped and flopped on the sand. He wished he knew what Wilson was planning and how much time they had.

"Did you hear this rat telling Dietrich we were mice?" Hitch asked Tully.

"Said we wasn't worth the trouble of going after," Tully drawled.

"Think we should do him in now?" Hitch asked.

"Why sure, then we'll go back to Dietrich and make him a Rat Patrol," Tully said. "He knows who counts for what."

"That Sergeant Troy doesn't count for beans, not any more," Hitch said. "He's dead, Moffitt and he. We're on our own."

"Out of the mouths of babes," Troy said with a smile. "That's right, Hitch. You're on your own. You and Tully get into camp and report to Wilson. I don't care if he's in bed, get him out and tell him the grade is the safe passage. Give him what you've got on the mortars and anything else. I'll tell you what Moffitt and I found on the ridge. You saw where his armor is parked. Moffitt and I will try to get back sometime today."

"You're going after Moffitt now?" Hitch asked.

"That's right," Troy said and got to his feet. "Come with me another ten minutes and then head for camp."

Troy described the cannon and the 75s, the two antitank guns and the location of the weapons as they trotted south.

"Do a little squatting and bobbing up and down," he told Tully and Hitch when they turned east, "just for the lieutenant's benefit if he still can see, so he won't catch on one of us is missing."

The ridge was jagged and the embankment steep. Troy

131

crossed the desert toward the ragged stone on his stomach. The Jerries would have no reason for mining this area, he told himself, because no tank could mount that wall. But his mouth was dry and his forehead wet before he reached the foot of the escarpment. He tottered to his feet and hugged the wall as he trotted south, watching for the concealed trail the substitute Rat Patrol had taken. He had not been running five minutes when he stumbled on it, a narrow pathway that entered the stone wall through a fissure. He saw footprints in the sand and unhesitatingly turned onto the path. He walked cautiously now, watching the prints that led downward, the ones left by the two privates who had been lucky. When he came to a place where the thinning sand was trampled and dark splotches stained the trail, he hoisted himself up the knife-edged outcrops and crawled like a skink over the stone. This was no way to treat civilian clothing, he told himself, but he couldn't work much humor into the thought.

Slipping, gripping hard blades of stone to hold the distance he'd gained, kicking for toeholds on the sheer face, he clawed his way up. Below to his right the trail was flat and slanted like a ramp through ragged fissures toward the top, but he saw the holes in it the mines had made. When he had scaled the embankment to a shelf an easy arm's length from the crest, he toppled on his face and lay panting and bleeding. His heart pumped furiously and his head spun. His suit was ripped and his shoes were gouged. Just above, he heard the heavy tread of boots. They stopped and he held his breath, afraid the gasps would reveal him. He was utterly spent and unable to resist. The boots crunched away. It was almost half an hour before the footfalls returned and then he was ready for the guard.

Like an animal, he crouched for the kill, knife in hand, muscles coiled, thought shut off. The footsteps stopped again. A match flared as the guard paused to light a cigarette. Troy sprang from the ledge, gripping the guard by the neck in the vise of his arm, plunging his knife into his belly and ripping it open with a savage upward slash. He rolled and lay with the guard's neck in the crook of his arm until he was sure the man was dead. In those seconds, he examined this area of the ridge. He could see no guns and there was neither place nor reason for them here. A path disappeared between the stones a few yards north. To the east was the drop to the desert. To the west, rock spires.

Troy wiped his knife on his trousers, took the guard's machine pistol and walked warily up the path. The trail passed through clefts and he had shadows where he flattened against the walls and listened. He slunk for almost a mile before he heard footsteps. Backing away, he waited in darkness, ready to pounce. A guard stepped into the trough where the moonlight was shaded. He was casual, unconcerned and unprepared. Troy's fingers and his knife choked the cry that bubbled in his throat.

Beyond, the ridge flattened and Troy saw the row of cannon and rocket launchers that commanded the desert. A few men of the gun crews sat and smoked but most stretched on the ground and slept. Troy went to the ground and pulled himself with his elbows and knees toward a row of halftracks that had been backed well off the rim. He felt as if he'd fallen off a cliff and was certain that he looked it.

Crawling under the fronts of the halftracks, he reached the area of the ridge beyond the top of the grade. From here he could see Dietrich's tent. It was only about thirty yards from the halftrack under which he lay. Light from the acetylene lantern spilled through the opening. The rest of the ridge was lighted by the moon. He waited, watching and listenin . A guard walked out from the shadows between the two tanks and past the Hispano-Suiza, lingering at the car. Troy wondered whether he could back the car between the tanks as Tully had suggested. The guard drifted by the halftrack, almost aimlessly. Troy waited long minutes until the man returned on his patrol and disappeared behind the tanks. Then he sprang to his feet and darted toward the tent.

He ran crouching for the back of the tent. As he reached it and stopped in the shadow close to the wall, he heard the sound of Moffitt's voice but not the words. Dietrich laughed; boisterously, Troy thought. He hoped Moffitt was keeping Dietrich's glass filled with bourbon. Troy waited.

Except for Dietrich and Moffitt, no one was stirring in the area. Troy held the machine pistol in his right hand and
133

lifted the knife in his left to slit the canvas. A rustle, the merest whisper of a noise brushed his ear and he whirled gripping the knife tightly as he brought his left hand to his hip. Grosse faced him scarcely not more than a yard away and the machine pistol in his hands was pointed at Troy's stomach.

18

By the time Peilowski returned to HQ with two medics both Albright and Kierzek were suffering from shock. Their teeth chattered and they shivered. Then, alternately they were bathed with perspiration as they burned with fever. Wilson had wrapped both of them in blankets and bathed their faces when they flushed. One medic went with scissors directly to Kierzek's leg while the other prepared to give them morphine. They had brought one stretcher.

"What are the facilities at the aid station?" Wilson asked as he stepped aside. "Are there cots?"

"No, sir," the dark-haired medic with the scissors said without looking up. "We're prepared for field dressing only prior to evacuation."

"What will you do with these men?" Wilson demanded. "They're wounded seriously and they're obviously suffering from shock."

"Best we can do is leave them on stretchers, elevate them off the ground with a couple cartridge cases," the light-haired medic with the hypo said.

"Peilowski," Wilson ordered. "Go to the truck and get your cot and blankets. These men will sleep here tonight."

"Yes, sir," the first sergeant said quickly and turned to leave the tent, but not before Wilson noted that his face was flushing.

"How badly are they wounded?" Wilson asked as the light-haired medic swabbed Albright's temple and cheek and the other probed Kierzek's leg.

"This fellow caught a good chunk of scrap against his shin," the dark-haired one said. "There's a fracture. He's been walking on it and we've got some bone fragments punching through the skin. I'll clean it, shake some sulpha powder on it, bandage it lightly and splint it, but he needs treatment fast. Can you evacuate him by air?"

"I'll arrange it at once," Wilson said crisply. "How about the other?"

"Lacerations, superficial wounds on his temple. Possible fracture of the cheekbone. Possibly shrapnel imbedded in the skull. I can't tell. He needs out."

"All right, do what you can to make them comfortable," Wilson said. "I'll have an aircraft in to take them out as soon as it's light enough to land."

He ran to the communications van. Kalmuk was on duty and the Eskimo got the message off to Bir el Alam without delay. Wilson's request was confirmed immediately.

Peilowski was setting up his cot on the opposite side of the tent from Wilson's when he stepped back into the tent. The medics had cut Kierzek's fatigues away and wiped him with alcohol. They wrapped him in a blanket, lifted him to Wilson's cot atnd covered him with a second blanket. When they had stripped and bathed Albright, they wrapped him and placed him on Peilowski's cot. The dark-haired medic picked up the stretcher and they stepped toward the opening.

"Oh, Doc," Wilson said absently. "Leave that stretcher behind. Peilowski can scrounge some cases and I'll sleep on it tonight."

The dark-haired medic's hesitancy was scarcely enough to notice and Wilson thought nothing of it. He put the stretcher back on the ground and the two medics walked off without another word.

Peilowski's face was growing red when Wilson glanced at him and he was trying to contain his laughter.

135

"What is it, Peilowski?" Wilson asked curtly. "I do
see much humor in this ward."

"Sorry, sir," Peilowski said, trying hard to be serious
bursting out in a belly laugh. "It's just that the medics c
got two stretchers and they been using them themselve;
sleep on. I was wondering whose bed you took a
tonight."

Peilowski found two empty wooden cases and set
stretcher up on them outside the tent for Wilson. The
took his .45 and a flashlight, placed them inside the bo:
his head, rolled a GI blanket from his locker around
fatigues, and lay down. He looked once at the starry
and was asleep.

Violent oaths, a string of epithets, shrill and
splitting, awakened him. He struggled with the blanket
bound him like a mummy cloth, threw it off, reached
his pistol and flashlight and sat up, beaming the light at
babble. Two wild-eyed, tousle-haired men with barb
mustaches were struggling with two guards. The foreig
were dressed in civilian clothing. Each time the gua
jabbed them with their tommy guns the men went int
frenzy.

"Good lord, now what!" Wilson shouted, soun
angry. "First the Arabs and now the Ey-tees. Don't tell
You caught them spying for the Jerries."

"Babbuino!" the man in the purple suit spat him. I
never heard a word uttered with such defiance.

"If I knew what he said, I don't think I'd like it," Wi
said patiently. He examined the prisoners. They wer
disreputable a pair as he'd encountered. He could alr
find it in his heart to wish the guard would shoot s
villains instead of bringing them to him, he thought,
membering Albright and Kierzek in the tent and Mer
and Heath scattered over the trail. Harshly he asked,
either of you men know who in camp speaks Italian? I
pose I'll have to interrogate these monsters."

"Waddaya mean, monster?" the ruffian in the purple
and pink shirt screeched.

"Waddaya mean, spik Italiano?" the cutthroat in
brown gabardine suit and brown shirt screamed.

"We spikka da Inglis," purple suit sneered, lifting

136

wicked mustache. "*Fantoccio!* Waddaya wanta know, ya beega *babbo?*"

"Now, see here!" Wilson said, enraged. He started to stand. The stretcher slipped off the box at his head and he sprawled in the sand.

"Geeva look, Sol!" purple suit cried delightedly. "He's-a no *babbo,* he's-a *bimbo*. He wanta crawl, the creep!"

Wilson jumped to his feet, quivering with wrath. "Now you men be quiet!" he hollered. "I will not tolerate your ridicule. What are you men doing here?"

"Watsa wrong, thees place?" brown suit asked. "Oh ho, you not got room, all full-a up tonight. Hokay, we go see Meestair Dietrich. Maybe he geev us room weeth bath."

"What do you know about Dietrich?" Wilson yelled in blind rage at these insufferable idiots who baited him so mercilessly.

"He send-a us," purple suit said with a shrug. "He say, 'You keel that Heetch and Tooley, by dam' I pay for that.'"

"What! Why you—!" Wilson felt his eyes widening and his jaw going slack. I must not lose my dignity, he thought, but he knew it was no use as he bent over, convulsed with silent laughter.

Then it rolled out. He roared. He howled. He wept. He laughed until he hurt and sat weakly on the stretcher. Except the stretcher wasn't there any more and that was funny too. To hell with the dignity for once, he thought, sitting on the sand holding his sides and thinking of the two guards standing there watching their CO who, they must be certain, had lost his marbles. That set him off in fresh peals.

Finally exhausted, Wilson shakily got to his feet. "Heetch, Tooley, is this what G2 decided to do? What have they done to you? Who is which?"

Purple suit said, "Private Mark Hitchcock, reporting for duty as ordered, sir."

And brown suit said, "Private Tully Pettigrew, reporting for duty as commanded, *babbo*."

"Um, yes," Wilson said, trying to make his face and voice stern. "I must make a note of those terms. Perhaps I could run through a summary court-martial. By the way, what do they mean? What does *babbo* mean?"

"I didn't call you that, Hitch did," Tully said. "It means pop, dad, pa."

"I've been called worse," Wilson said with a smile. He glanced at the dumbfounded guards. "It's all right, men. You may go back to your posts. It's just half the Rat Patrol reporting back." And to Hitch and Tully, "Come along. We'll go to your quarters and you can fill me in. There are two hospital cases in the tent."

He told them briefly of the Arab's treachery and the tragic fate of the men who had worn the Rat Patrol's headpieces.

"We suspected something like that from what we heard," Hitch said. "There was an Arab squatting outside Dietrich's tent when we left tonight. I'll bet it was the same one. Come to collect."

"I only hope we encounter him once more," Wilson said vengefully.

He had taken along the gas lantern, maps, paper and pencils. In the cavern under the camouflage net with the lantern glaring on the sand between the jeeps, Hitch called the weapons and their positions while Wilson charted them and Tully heated water over a cardboard fire for coffee. The day had been difficult, men had lost their lives, the test firing of the missiles in the morning would mark a crucial phase of the battle, yet Wilson could not help chuckling now and then as he looked at his thoroughly disreputable Tully and Hitch.

"The safe passage is the grade," Hitch concluded. "Apparently they had just the one mine planted on it. We walked down it tonight."

They would saturate the ridge and slope with fire from the new weapon, Wilson thought. They would concentrate the fire on either side of the grade and he would send the column straight on up before the Jerries had recovered from their shock.

"What about Troy and Moffitt?" he asked absently when the last detail down to the position of Dietrich's armored column had been noted. They both were perfectly all right, of course, or Hitch and Tully would have told him at once. "Where are they?"

He saw Hitch look up sharply at Tully as the coffee was handed out. Despite their disguises, he recognized the

138

quick look of concern that passed between them.

"Dietrich held Moffitt hostage against our return," Hitch said. "Troy went back to try and rescue him."

"Oh," Wilson said. He didn't feel like laughing any more. He felt very old and tired.

19

Grosse was no soldier, and he never would be. You don't stand within reach of even an unarmed man and point the barrel of a gun at his stomach. It is too easy to grasp and thrust away. When a man is armed, as Troy was armed with a machine pistol and a knife, you must stand well away or the odds are not at all in your favor. Troy reacted to the confrontation behind Dietrich's tent like lightning. He smashed the barrel of his machine pistol against Grosse's wrist and before the Jerry could yelp with pain, rammed it into Grosse's gut. Grosse dropped his weapon and doubled over, gasping. Another blow with the machine pistol, this time at the base of Grosse's skull and the persistent and brave but foolish orderly was out cold.

Troy had no way of knowing whether the sound of the brief but violent action had reached inside the tent. The knife still was clenched in his left hand and he rent the canvas with a swift slash. As he thrust his way through the slit, he saw that Moffitt had done his part and kept Dietrich's glass well filled. Dietrich staggered to his feet and started to smile when he recognized Sam Enna. Moffitt chopped him down with a judo blow behind his ear. Dietrich collapsed limply on the sand.

"Get the car, Jack," Troy said calmly. "Bring it around to the tent, facing west. Stroll, don't run. Only Doeppler

139

and Grosse know our status here and they're both taken care of."

"T'anks fer de timely entry," Moffitt said. "I'd just said 'Right-o' but Captain Dietrich was a bit poshed and thought I was being funny." He left the tent in a leisurely fashion.

Troy removed Dietrich's pistol from the holster and thrust it in his waist band before he grasped the floppy form under the armpits and hiked it into the camp chair. Dietrich's eyes were open and glazed. His head lolled on his chest and he looked very drunk. Troy adjusted the chair in front of the table so it was facing the entrance and tilted a glass of brandy between Dietrich's fingers so some of the liquor slopped out. He stepped to the side of the entrance and inspected his handiwork critically. Very drunk, indeed, he appraised with satisfaction. Let *Herr Hauptmann* Hans Dietrich explain that tomorrow.

The car idled quietly close to the opening. Troy knelt to slip through the front door that Moffitt opened. He turned for a final look at Dietrich. He was a masterpiece.

"Hold it, Jack," Troy said. "I've got an idea."

He ran to Dietrich, seized him under the armpits again, pulled him off the chair and hauled him to the running board. He straddled the inert body and hoisted it onto the front seat, bracing the feet against the floorboard and propping the back against the seat.

"Got to get his cap," he said, breathing heavily with his effort. "Your violin case still in there?"

"Under the table," Moffitt said.

Troy found Dietrich's cap on his locker, grabbed the violin case and snatched the half empty bottle of bourbon from the table. Moffitt had swung open the back door and Troy dived onto the floor with the machine pistol, violin case, bottle and Dietrich's cap. He tossed the cap over the seat.

"Make him look natural, Jack," he said, watching the back of Dietrich's head as the high-peaked cap was fitted.

Troy closed the door, the front door slammed and the car glided smoothly away in second gear. He could hear the sand trickling from the tread of the big tires and then the steel walls of the tanks closed on either side. Troy felt himself squeezing his arms against his ribs to help provide

140

more space and smiled quickly. He was feeling good. Then the tanks were behind them and there was open space all around and the vast blue night sky above pricked with a million tiny stars.

"Stillstand!" a voice commanded harshly from ahead and Troy saw reflected illumination as Moffitt switched on his lights.

The car slowed. Troy pushed to his knees and flipped the machine pistol off safety. From the corners of his eyes, he saw Dietrich turn his head. *"Rechnung bezahlen!"* Dietrich barked.

"Herr Hauptmann!" the voice said, close at hand and respectful.

The car spurted down the back slope of the ridge. Troy sat on the floor with his spine against the seat and leveled the Browning automatic at the back of Dietrich's head.

"I've got a gun on you, Dietrich," he said tightly. "Just keep on cooperating and it won't go off." He drew in his breath, still puzzled. "Jack, when did he come to? What have you got, a pistol or a knife in his side?"

Moffitt chuckled and Dietrich's head flopped forward. "Neither," he said. "I just turned on the headlamps and manipulated with my elbow while the guard was half blind. The voice you heard was mine. Poor old Dietrich is colder than last night's mackerel."

"Good work, Jack," Troy said, laughing and putting the Browning in his coat pocket. "That evens the score."

"What do you propose to do with the blighter?" Moffitt asked.

"I don't know," Troy called. The car was bouncing on rough ground. "It was a last minute idea."

"For not knowing, it was an inspiration," Moffitt said. "We'll not be bothered for a bit. If anyone asks, that guard will report that Dietrich went out to take the air with his civilian friend."

"Are we clear?" Troy asked. He was being jostled and tossed on the floor. "Is it okay to get onto the seat?"

"Why not wait until we get to the road," Moffitt suggested. "There's no reason why anyone should watch us through binoculars, but you never know."

"I ought to grab Dietrich's cap and change places with him," Troy growled.

141

He started to push aside the cans and handbags, the violin case and machine pistol to make himself more comfortable. As he piled the handbags, he remembered someone had found a sweater in his handbag. Hitch. A woolen sweater with a turtleneck. He inspected the tags in the flame of his lighter, found M. Enna's and unzipped it. The sweater was on top and felt soft but thick and warm. He yanked it out and threw it on the seat. After he'd emptied his coat pockets, he wadded it and threw it over the gasoline cans. The necktie and silk shirt followed. He dug the toilet kit from the handbag, took the bar of soap and sloshed a little water from a can into one palm. Gripping the can between his knees, he washed his hands and face as thoroughly as he could, using a palmful of water at a time. He found the towel, dried, and pulled the sweater over his head. There was a comb in the kit and he ran it through his hair, digging at his scalp to relieve the itch. When he'd tucked the sweater into his waistband, he shoved the two pistols into his belt which already supported his sheathed knife. He felt almost human but distinctly foreign.

The car rolled onto a smoother surface and picked up speed. Wind whistled coldly about his ears.

"Sit up if you like," Moffitt called. "We're on the road."

Troy sat with his back against the side and his legs stretched out. He looked back. No one was following. He lighted a cigarette and settled comfortably. He had been filled with apprehensions about this mission and it had been a breeze. They'd even captured Dietrich. It was odd but that didn't make him particularly happy.

"You know, old boy," Moffitt called. "It's going to be a bit sticky, managing a prisoner. We've quite a trip ahead and the only way we shall carry on is for one to sleep while the other drives."

Troy laughed heartily. "We'll have to tie him up."

"It's either that or sit with a gun pointed at the blighter," Moffitt said gloomily.

"Why don't you come right out and say it, Jack?" Troy said. "Who will there be to make life interesting if Dietrich is in a POW camp?"

"Such a thought would horrify Wilson," Moffitt said. "We can't simply chuck him nor permit him to escape."

"No," Troy agreed. "But there is one thing that would

make Dietrich suffer more than being taken prisoner," Troy said.

"Yes?" Moffitt said, sounding amused. "Expound, please. You interest me."

"It demoralizes him when people laugh at him," Troy said. "It pains him physically."

"Go on, Troy," Moffitt said. "It's your show."

"When you come to the trail that leads by that ravine where we holed up yesterday, turn onto it," Troy said.

"Yes?" Moffitt said.

"We left the camouflage net cached there with some food. We'd better pick up the net. I think we can leave Dietrich there. It's about fifty miles from the ridge. We'll stretch him out and stack the food and wine beside him. He won't starve, but he'll have a long hike. Depending on what Wilson has in mind, maybe by the time Dietrich starts up the road, what's left of his column will pick him up on its way to Tunisia."

"Umm, interesting, Troy," Moffitt said, laughing quietly. "I'd like to be around when he awakens, wonders where he is and how he arrived."

Moffitt turned off his headlights and drove at a steady fifty miles an hour. Troy glanced at Dietrich from time to time. The Jerry's head joggled with the motion of the car. Moffitt's blow, combined with the whiskey Dietrich had drunk, seemed to have been too much for him.

It was about one hour after Moffitt and Troy had left the Jerry camp when Moffitt swung the Hispano-Suiza onto the hardpacked trail, drove a mile toward the sea, and turned onto the stone. He went into second gear for the descent to the dry bed and crawled along it to the ravine. It was deeply shadowed and he used the searchlight as he backed into it.

"Leave it on," Troy called, jumping out and running back toward the pile of stones he'd left over the net. Everything was intact and he lugged the cumbersome bundle toward the searchlight, looking down at his pointed shoes so it wouldn't blind him. "Give me a hand, Jack," he called as he neared the car. "I'll unroll the net and you can pick out the food. Then we'll carry Dietrich out and leave him."

He looked up as the door slammed and Moffitt walked into the beam. He thought Jack was moving a little stiffly

143

and laughed. "Tightening up already?" Troy asked. The remark apparently piqued Moffitt because he didn't answer.

"You may stop there and turn around, Sergeant Moffitt," Dietrich said. "Don't move, Sergeant Troy. I am behind the spotlight and Sergeant Moffitt will tell you that I have his submachine gun."

Troy had dropped the net and stood with his arms dangling at his sides.

"Sorry, old boy," Moffitt murmured. "I stepped out to get the violin case from the rear and he knocked me down. I had no idea that he was feigning."

"The deception was brilliant, Sergeant Troy," Dietrich said. "It is too bad you permitted your compassion and childish sense of humor to overwhelm your judgment. You know, I was not amused at your plans for me. Now loosen your belt and allow your weapons to fall to the ground."

Troy obeyed in a daze. He unbuckled the belt and the two pistols fell between his feet.

"Remove the knife sheath and drop it," Dietrich commanded.

Troy did as he was told.

"Step back ten paces," Dietrich said.

Moffitt and Troy backed away. Dietrich stepped into the light. His machine gun was trained on them and his face was pale with fury.

"I enjoyed your performance, Sergeant Troy," Dietrich said. Troy was emerging from the shock that had numbed his mind. He detected a note of barely contained frenzy in Dietrich's voice. His wrath at what they'd done and planned to do was overcoming him. "You really are a much better actor than soldier," Dietrich went on. "It is really a shame that the world should never have the opportunity to witness your act. You might have lived to play another day if you had not indulged yourself in your fancy for games. You do not seem to realize that this is war, Sergeant Troy, uncompromising, unremitting war. There is no place for jokes and tricks and unfortunately for you I have not enjoyed your pranks."

Dietrich kept his eyes and gun on Moffitt and Troy as he stooped to pick up the pistols and knife.

144

"Break!" Troy said sharply and plunged away from the spotlight. He felt Moffitt dive in the other direction. The machine gun rattled and the bullets ricocheted on the walls of the ravine. The bursts arced over a hundred and eighty degrees. Troy scrabbled along the side of the car. The machine gun was firing wildly in all directions. Troy crawled under the high-wheeled automobile and saw Dietrich's boots running toward him. Instead of backing out, Troy pushed ahead to meet them. The spotlight swept the ravine as Dietrich stood at the car and manipulated it. Troy slammed his arm around the boots, hugging and jerking. The machine gun blasted and fell as Dietrich slapped the ground with his face. Moffitt and Troy swarmed over him and Moffitt knocked him out again with a judo chop at the base of the skull.

"No chances this time," Troy panted. "What have we got to tie him up?"

"Not a thing," Moffitt said, standing apart and holding the pistol on Dietrich. Troy retrieved the Browning, submachine gun and knife.

"There's the net," Troy said. "We'll roll him in that and tuck in the edges. He'll never get out."

"That is quite all right with me," Moffitt said angrily. "The chap was becoming quite hysterical."

Troy dumped the provisions from the net. They rolled Dietrich onto it, brought the ends over his head and feet and turned him over and over for the length of the net. Moffitt took the head and Troy the feet and they carted their trussed prisoner to the car and heaved him onto the back seat.

"It was the hysteria that gave us a chance," Troy said, picking up the scattered cans and sausage. He carried them to the trunk and stowed them away. "He was wild; his shooting was wild. If he'd been himself we wouldn't have had time to make a break."

Moffitt lifted a can of gasoline from the floor and poured it in the tank. He put water in the radiator. Troy picked up the bottle of wine that had been in the net and placed it on the front seat.

"Do you think he planned to shoot us here?" Moffitt asked, looking about the ravine.

"Not before we ran," Troy said. "I think he planned to

get into the back seat, have us drive him back to the ridge and then put us on trial just the way we're rigged out as spies. We'd have ended up shot dead, but it would have been by a firing squad."

"The man told us war is not a game," Moffitt remarked.

"The man is right," Troy said soberly. "Killing isn't fun. We don't like it, but Dietrich's people let a silly-looking little madman with a toothbrush mustache hoodwink them into thinking they could run the world, and we're fighting for survival. Dietrich yaks about jokes and pranks, but he misses the point. If you can laugh a man to death, why shoot him?"

Troy climbed behind the steering wheel. Moffitt darted a look at Dietrich and stepped into the front seat from the other side. Troy let out the clutch and the car wheeled out of the ravine and climbed effortlessly to the stone. Troy switched off the spotlight and drove the mile to the road without talking. It was not his place to try nor judge, and personal feelings should not influence the discharge of his duties. Yet there were times when a man must make his own decisions, answering to himself as well as accepting the consequences of his actions. Troy did not hesitate when the car approached the road. He turned east, back toward the Jerry camp, and tromped the throttle. The big car soared.

"You have decided not to take the prisoner in to Wilson," Moffitt asked.

"I have decided this is a better way of punishing him," Troy said. "The Jerries don't have many opportunities for a belly laugh."

20

It was oh-three-hundred in the morning when Doeppler's head dropped to his chest and he jerked awake. He groaned at the chill that had crept into his bones. His eyes ached dully and he closed them for a moment. When he opened them again he saw that it was very dark. The moon was down and only a few stars remained in the sky. They glimmered feebly. It was impossible to see anything on the desert. Two of the men with him in the machine gun pit were asleep. Only Krafft, the apple-cheeked boy who wore glasses and spoke English, was awake.

"They have not returned?" Doeppler asked him. The lieutenant straightened his spine and felt a stab in his kidneys. It was very cold and the ground was hard. He was spent. Except for the small catnaps he had stolen, he had not slept for forty-eight hours.

"I have watched faithfully," Krafft said earnestly. "Although the morning is dark, if anything had moved I would have seen it. My eyes see well in darkness."

"Yes, that is why I asked you to watch for me," Doeppler said, although he acknowledged to himself this was not the truth. He knew very well he would have fallen asleep at the post.

"Something has gone wrong," Doeppler said mournfully. He did not want to admit the assassination the American gangsters had undertaken could have misfired. He would have to carry the report to Captain Dietrich and bear the brunt of his ire. He sighed. "They have had time to murder a battalion. I am afraid they have been captured." He stood on wobbly legs. "I must tell my conclusions to

Captain Dietrich. You and the others remain. If the men should con e back, hold them at the bottom and send one of the others for me."

"I shall remain alert," Krafft said, glancing at the two who slept. He sounded disdainful.

Doeppler moved cautiously behind the machine gun nests and rifle positions that pocked the slope above the minefield. Most of the crews were huddled within great-coats and sleeping, but a few of the men were awake and one challenged him. Doeppler crossly told him to go back to sleep and plodded on. He turned wearily up the grade, wishing only that he could wrap a blanket about himself and close his eyes.

He could see that a lantern still burned in Dietrich's tent as soon as he mounted the ridge and he ordered his legs to move more quickly. His boots felt as if they had flatirons attached to the soles and he could scarcely lift his feet from the ground. Once he stumbled. The captain would be in a vile humor, waiting in his camp chair behind his table. Doeppler shivered at thought of the outburst his report would provoke. He wondered what extra duty he would be assigned, but he managed a very military stiff-armed salute as he marched into the tent.

Dietrich was not seated behind the table. Someone was sprawled uncovered on the cot but it was not Dietrich. Doeppler rolled the man over on his back and sucked in his breath. It was Grosse, sleeping on the captain's bed! Grosse must be drunk, he thought in horror. He shook him by the shoulders and slapped his face but the man did not come out of his stupor.

When Doeppler went to the washstand at the back of the tent for water, he saw the rent in the canvas. He stood rooted for a moment, examining the tent. There was no evidence of violence. But there was the rip in the canvas, Grosse sleeping or insensible on Dietrich's cot and Dietrich vanished, along with the American hoodlum who had re-mained behind.

Two glasses, one still containing a liquid that looked like tea, were on the table. Doeppler picked it up and sniffed it. It was not tea nor Scotch whisky or brandy. The aroma was pleasant and tempted him. He glanced furtively around as if someone might be watching from a corner, then lifted the

148

glass to his lips, bending his head and tossing the drink off in a gulp. The liquor seemed harsh and seared his throat, but it warmed his chest and stomach and he imagined he felt much better at once.

Doeppler poured a little water into a basin, took a towel and knelt beside the cot, feeling for Grosse's pulse as he wet the towel and squeezed drops of water on his face. The pulse was steady and no marks showed on Grosse's face so he must be drunk, Doeppler thought, confirming his first suspicion. Grosse did not respond and Doeppler became agitated. He soaked the towel and wrung it until the water streamed over Grosse's eyelids and ran down his cheeks. Doeppler began to tremble, obsessed with the idea of getting Grosse out of the tent before Dietrich came back. He was certain Dietrich somehow would blame him for Grosse's outrageous conduct. He saw that he was dribbling water onto Dietrich's blanket.

"You lout, you oaf!" he cried and rolled Grosse off the cot onto the sand. He thought he heard a hollow moan, but it may have been Grosse's stomach emitting alcoholic fumes. Running to the washstand, he seized the pitcher and hurled half its contents in Grosse's face.

Grosse opened his eyes for a moment and the lids closed again. Doeppler was beside himself. He flung the rest of the water in Grosse's face and beat at it with the wet towel. After a monumental struggle, Grosse managed to sit up.

"Are you out of your mind?" Doeppler yelled. Now that Grosse had recovered part of his senses, the lieutenant's fears turned to wrath. "To get drunk and lose your wits on the captain's bed!"

"The captain!" Grosse was distressed. He tottered to his feet and reached to Doeppler's shoulder for support. "Where is the captain? They have taken the captain away," he sobbed and tears streamed down his cheeks. "I tried to warn the captain, but he would not listen. The Rat Patrol has made off with the captain."

"Grosse, you are disgustingly drunk," Doeppler said in complete revulsion. "I should have left you on the cot for the captain to discover."

"Lieutenant, I beg of you to listen," Grosse gasped. "You know I do not drink. I have been severely beaten. Here, see for yourself." He jerked the shirt from his

149

trousers and Doeppler saw a great welt that was beginning to discolor above the navel. "That makes me ill. I want to vomit," Grosse said. "And here." He pulled back his cuff. A knot bunched on the wrist. He bent his head and touched the top of his spine. "Feel here, but gently." Doeppler found a swelling as large as half a golf ball. "When I recovered consciousness, I crawled into the tent to warn the captain once more but he was not here. Already they had seized him. I could go no further and collapsed on the cot."

"Get hold of yourself, man," Doeppler said sharply. Worries crowded his mind and pushed one another about. "Who beat you?"

"The one who called himself Sam Enna, the big man with the gold tooth who talked all the time," Grosse said breathlessly. "I discovered him about to slit the back of the tent with a knife and pointed my machine pistol at him. He also had a machine pistol and before I knew what was happening, he was whipping me with it. I must have fallen unconscious. When I recovered I was on the ground. I pulled myself into the tent and it was empty."

"It was not the Rat Patrol," Doeppler said, stalling for time, wondering what he ought to do. "Two of them are dead, the other two badly wounded. It was the Enna brothers. I distrusted them from the moment I took them prisoners."

"Call the men anything you wish," Grosse said desperately. "The one called Jack who remained here and the one called Sam who came back and attacked me have captured the captain. You must do something." He stumbled to the entrance and looked out. "I do not see the car. They have driven away with Captain Dietrich."

This was terrible, Doeppler thought miserably, to happen when he was officer of the guard. He pushed Grosse aside at the opening, stood outside the tent and bawled at the top of his voice for the guard stationed beyond the tanks on the route to the road.

"Wolke!" And again: "Wolke!" And yet again: "Wolke!"

A heavily bundled figure ran toward the tent from between two tanks. Other men appeared from nowhere and drifted toward Doeppler.

"What is it? What is the trouble?" Wolke huffed. He was middle-aged with gray hair under his cap and deep lines in his ruddy face.

"Did Captain Dietrich leave camp in the touring automobile with the bareheaded men who looked like Italians?" Doeppler asked. Half a dozen men now had formed a half circle around the front of the tent and others were trotting up.

"He left with one of the men driving," Wolke said. "I saw the car coming out between the tanks without lights and not knowing who was in it, ordered the car to halt. It turned its lights on and slowed. As it passed, the captain turned to me saying to clear the way and the car went on in the direction of the road. It was nearing midnight."

"One man only in the car with the captain?" Doeppler asked.

"One man only that I saw," Wolke said. "There could have been half a dozen lying in the back. It is a very large automobile."

"You are certain it was the captain and he told you to clear the way?" Doeppler asked.

"That is so," Wolke said, "and it made me wonder. It was not like Captain Dietrich to speak like that to me. I have been in the Army more than twenty years and he had a certain respect for the regulars. It is not impossible there was a gun against his ribs."

"He would not have gone with them alone," Grosse spoke up. "He does not trust anyone. He would not have gone willingly. They have seized him. We must go after them."

Doeppler felt wretchedly sick. Whatever he did would be wrong. If Dietrich had been spirited away by the Americans, it would be his fault. If he had departed with them freely on some mission and he went chasing after them, Dietrich would be furious. More men had come up. They stood, silent and waiting.

"They should have returned if they were coming back," Doeppler said. "We will look for a ways. It is possible they have ruptured a tire or need other help. Grosse, bring up the captain's staff car. Wolke, get a personnel carrier." About a dozen men had crowded around and he spoke to them. "Men, get your weapons and report back at once."

151

Grosse and Wolke trotted away for the vehicles and the men dispersed. Doeppler moved unhappily about the tent. The three American gangsters had not returned from the American camp. According to Grosse, one of them, Sam, had managed to slip back. There was the rip in the canvas to support Grosse. Wolke confirmed Dietrich had left in the car with at least one of them. With a start of a good three hours, the car could be halfway to the Allied lines. Worst of all, the car could have come from the Allied lines across the ridge the night before. He had not seen two jeeps as he had reported to Dietrich but only the single spotlight from a distance. Thoroughly miserable, he went to Dietrich's locker. It was open and he took a bottle of brandy, gulping several swallows and shoving the bottle in his pocket. Either way, it would make little difference.

He heard motors idling and went out. Half a dozen of the men had returned. They climbed into the truck and Doeppler sat in the staff car with Grosse. The lights flared out and then were contained in the alley between the tanks. Doeppler turned and behind the truck scraped through. Grosse drove past the armored column and down the long, rocky slope toward the road. Doeppler pulled out the bottle and had another drink.

"The captain won't like that," Grosse said peevishly.

"We aren't going to find him," Doeppler said moodily. He felt as gloomy as the dark of morning.

"I warned him and he wouldn't listen," Grosse said and retched. Doeppler looked at him in alarm, but he swallowed and did not get sick.

"I know," Doeppler said sympathetically. "Unless he had the idea first, he was a hard man to convince."

"Don't talk about him as if he were dead already," Grosse said convulsively.

The headlights of the car spread over the road and Grosse started to turn onto it. Behind, the lights of the truck veered suddenly off to the right and the personnel carrier braked abruptly.

"Stop," Doeppler said. The men were jumping from the truck and running toward a large dark bundle that lay beside the grade. Doeppler swung out as Grosse slowed. He trotted, holding the bottle in his pocket with one hand and his machine pistol in the other. When he reached the

152

men, they were grouped around the bundle. It was a net. It squirmed and jumped and a steady stream of oaths flowed from it. The men had left a gap so the lights from the truck shone on it and revealed some kind of person deep inside. The men were beginning to laugh and make jokes.

"What does the net say?"

"The net has caught a talking fish."

"Perhaps it is a mermaid, although I have never heard a mermaid curse like that."

"It is Father Neptune. He is angry he was asleep and taken in the net."

"Perhaps it is not a net and a talking fish at all, but a cocoon with a worm inside."

"Well, I can crush the worm," one said, stepping forward and rolling the writhing net over once and again with the toe of his boot.

The oaths from the net were muffled but explicit. The men roared with laughter and slapped their legs.

Doeppler came out of shock and shuddered. He turned his back and hit the bottle hard. Grosse walked up.

"What is it?" he asked.

"Dietrich. In a net."

"Thank God, he's safe!" Grosse said fervently.

"We're not," Doeppler said, taking Grosse by the arm. "Come quickly. Let's drive back to camp."

Grosse jerked away. "Why don't they release him? What are they doing to him?"

The laughter was becoming boisterous. Doeppler took a deep breath and another pull at the bottle. He turned. The men were rolling the man bundled in the net one from the other. Each volley of curses from deep inside only made them laugh harder.

"Stop!" Doeppler shouted. "What are you doing? There is a man in the net. Unfasten it and let him out."

"That won't get you off, Doeppler," Grosse said nastily. "You were here when they started and you let them get away with it."

"I'll say you were here with me," Doeppler snarled. "We'd better stand together. Come along."

The men pulled back sullenly as Doeppler and Grosse ran to the net. "We'll each take one end and undo it, Grosse," Doeppler said.

Doeppler fumbled with his end and pulled it back.

"Oh Lord!" Grosse groaned. "He's all rolled up. We'll have to unroll the whole net."

"Let's get it started," Doeppler said heavily. "It's too bad but there's no other way."

Standing on a flap of the net, Doeppler and Grosse began turning the bundle over and over. It cursed steadily. The men began to laugh again. Half a dozen twists and Doeppler stopped for breath. He wanted a drink. He wanted to run. He wished he were a private on garbage detail. The bundle humped and began to turn itself. The men guffawed.

"All right, Grosse, let's get this poor fellow out of here," Doeppler said with a prayer.

Grosse glowered and the bundle swore.

Another half dozen gentle turns and Dietrich emerged. His face was white and his eyes were coals of fire. He stood with his feet apart, swaying dizzily from side to side. A single gasp rose from the men grouped about the net and trembled in the air. Doeppler closed his eyes. There was silence and it was awesome.

"Do you have the car, Grosse?" Dietrich asked at last.

"Yes, sir," Grosse said.

"We shall go to the camp at once. Doeppler, I want the name of each man who is here. If anyone tries to slip away, shoot him."

21

The sun was an hour above the horizon and had begun to burn the color from the sky when Troy stood the Hispano-Suiza on its nose, rolled it down the sharp embankment in second gear against smoking brake linings and pointed the long hood north toward the eastern edge of the salt marsh that protected Dietrich's southern flank. When he was out of the rocks on the sandy slope and on the desert flat that stretched unbroken for fifty miles to the Allied camp, he stopped. Moffitt lifted his head from the corner of the seat.

"Anything wrong?" he inquired.

"You just slept through a dive an airplane wouldn't try," Troy said and wiped the wet and grimy palms of his hands on his pants legs. "Water and gas stop. Find something tasty in the trunk. We'll eat on the run. We're only an hour from home, but we don't know when Dietrich was found or whether he has been able to call in aircraft."

"Quite," Moffitt said, swinging out the door. "I imagine the chap is a bit annoyed."

If they had left Dietrich behind in the ravine as he had planned or if they had thrown him in the back seat and taken him along, they'd be in camp right now. He did not regret his decision to dump the Jerry on his own doorstep in a scruffy package. It was a derisive gesture that not only would destroy Dietrich's effectiveness but shake the confidence and morale of the entire unit. He was convinced the Jerries would have less stomach for fighting when Wilson launched an attack because of the way they had treated Dietrich. And Dietrich would not have his mind on fighting either. Right now he'd rather remove the Rat Patrol from the face of the desert than win a campaign. That was fine for Wilson but a little rough on Moffitt and him.

When he'd serviced the car and was back on the sticking leather seat behind the steering wheel, he pushed the car to its limit. The speedometer wobbled forth and back between eighty-five and a hundred miles an hour. The wind screamed through the bullethole in the windshield and the dust hung like the trail of a meteor behind them. The desert was flat and smooth, unbroken by even an occasional wadi or dune. To the left now lay the salt marsh white and glittering like Christmas snow. The miles clicked off; another fifteen miles and they'd be reporting to Wilson. He began to think they'd make it.

Above the rush of the wind boring at his eardrums, he heard the scream of diving planes before Moffitt turned around and saw them. Ahead and to the sides no area

155

offered even partial protection and the only concealment lay in the treacherous salt marsh that would swallow them forever.

"Three Messerschmitts," Moffitt called. "Coming in fast and low to strafe. Tight formation. Almost wingtip to wingtip."

Concentrated fire, Troy thought, three times two 20 mm. cannon, two 7.9 mm. machine guns. Murder. Coming in from behind. Hunters who'd flown the way they'd taken over the ridge. Dietrich had called them in, ordered them to gun down the two men in the open touring car.

"How close?" Troy shouted.

"About a mile."

About twelve seconds, he thought. Don't give them time to change their course. One. Two. Three. Jam the brakes. Slew right. Second gear. Slam ahead. Get out of the path of the slugs that are hailing on the sand. The ME-109s streaked by off-target in a screaming hurricane of sand. Troy skidded and shot north.

"That won't work again," he called. "They'll spread out. Jump, Jack, and dig a hole. They'll go for the car."

Moffitt lifted the tommy gun. "If they're low enough, I might hit a gas tank."

"This is it!" Troy yelled angrily. "Don't try to be a hero. Take a dive."

"They're circling upstairs," Moffitt said calmly. "Opening the formation. They're going to come in from behind again. Oooops! Give it everything. Head straight on."

"What is it?" Troy hollered. "What are they doing?"

"We jumped them, Sam," Moffitt said exultantly. "Right out of the sun. Three beautiful Spitfires are on their tails. It's a dogfight. They can't get at us."

"How did the RAF get into this?" Troy asked and laughed shrilly.

"Shall we ask to see their orders?" Moffitt asked and his voice was higher pitched than normal.

The sound of the fighters and the pound of their weapons high above was faint in Troy's ears. The hum of the engine was loud. He didn't glance at the speedometer. He was shoving the accelerator through the floorboard.

"One of the Messerschmitts has broken off," Moffitt

156

called. "It's going to dive at us."

"Watch it, Jack. I'll try to shake it."

"There's a Spitfire on its tail. It's not closing. The 109 is too fast."

"Where is it now?" Troy shouted.

"Straight for us," Moffitt said.

Troy used both the foot brake and the hand brake. He spun the wheel. The car careened, rocking from side to side. He had it in second gear and pulled away fast in the opposite direction. The Messerschmitt pulled out of its dive and started to climb.

"The Spitfire was waiting," Moffitt said, voice rising again in excitement. "He's got it. He's got it. The 109 is going down. Straight down. Streaking smoke. There's the crash."

Troy slowed and circled, driving north again. He saw a mushroom of black smoke rising from the desert.

"Jerry will have his hands full now," Moffitt gloated. "There's a spare Spitfire and neither of the 109s knows when he's going to have it diving on him."

Just the same, Troy thought, we're getting out of here. He bounced the speedometer up to a hundred. Black Vs appeared on the shimmering sand a few miles away. "We're going to make it," he said.

"The Messerschmitts know it," Moffitt said. "They've leveled off and they're going back to Tunis. The Spits are hanging onto their tails. They can't catch them. There they go, over the ridge."

"Whew," Troy said, but he didn't slacken the speed. He heard the keening thunder of the Spitfires. The three of them dived and buzzed the car. Moffitt stood, clinging to the door with one hand and waving with the other.

"Our chaps," he said, sitting again. He sounded all choked up.

"I wonder where we got that kind of support," Troy said.

He rammed the car into the camp at a modest sixty miles an hour, waved at a guard, who gaped but did not challenge nor fire. Skidding behind the halftracks, he barreled toward Wilson's tent at fifty, braked and skidded to a fine, dramatic, dusty stop that showered HQ with sand.

157

Corporal Locke poked his head from the radio van and Wilson stepped from the tent. He looked from Moffitt to Troy.

"Good to see you," he said and smiled. "I'm guessing, but Troy is wearing the turtleneck sweater. Hitch and Tully prepared me for your appearances. I'm afraid they cost me my dignity. Come in and have some coffee while you tell me what you've been up to." He looked at his watch. "Oh-nine-oh-seven hundred. We have about an hour."

"Not that stuff you drink," Troy said. "Can your stomach stand a decent breakfast?"

They laid it out for Wilson: fresh oranges, a Westphalian ham, Swiss cheese, olives, Melba toast, American-style coffee with condensed milk.

"We salvaged the coffee, but Dietrich's orderly scrounged our tin of butter," Moffitt said.

"The best part of it is, the coffee is piping hot," Wilson said, glancing enviously at the Sterno stove.

Tully and Hitch came in for the briefing. They'd removed the contact lenses and wore their usual uniform, thin faded khakis, but they still were the Enna brothers with bristling black mustaches and curly black hair under their distinctive headpieces.

"You're a sight, Hitch," Troy said with a laugh. Hitch hadn't shaved and red stubble covered his chin and jawbone. "Why don't you take off the wig and mustache?"

"We can't get them off," Hitch said with a fierce scowl. "They haven't sent the solvent for the adhesive. My head is itching so I can't stand it. That's my sweater you're wearing. I'll trade you for the Walther."

Troy shook his head and saw Wilson glancing from his face to his waist where the butts of the Browning and the Walther P-38 showed above the belt. The Jerry knife dangled in a sheath. "I don't know whether I can explain you to Washington," he said. "We have a VIP coming in this morning."

"What's the deal?" Troy asked.

"Your story first," Wilson said. Peilowski had been sent to the airstrip and they all were sitting around Wilson's table.

Moffitt and Troy gave him a quick rundown on the events of the evening.

"Maybe we should have brought Dietrich in," Troy finished, "but I kept thinking how it would be with us if you were delivered in a bundle like that."

Tully and Hitch laughed openly.

Wilson's eyes twinkled and he smiled broadly but he said, "Eh? What's that? I'm afraid I wasn't listening. Well, I'm sure it wasn't important. There isn't much time and I want to tell you about the man who is coming and the weapon he is bringing." He laughed. "To tell you the truth, I actually don't know very much about either myself."

A civilian ordnance expert, he said, was coming to test a multiple missile launcher that would provide area saturation bombardment. Wilson actually knew little of the details, but Troy was happy they hadn't been told why the positions and nature of the weapons on the ridge were wanted. Knowing that Wilson was counting on the area saturation bombardment to provide a breakthrough for the armored column might have made them tense and overanxious.

"We'll coordinate our offensive with the missile test firing," Wilson said. "The armor is ready to go at a moment's notice. Do you think Dietrich will mine the safe passage now that he knows who you are?"

"It is possible," Moffitt said.

"He hasn't done it yet," Wilson said. "The grade is under observation."

"We hope we threw him so far off balance that all he'll think about is getting back at us," Troy said. "Those Messerschmitts this morning were after the Hispano-Suiza and Moffitt and me. They had no other target. Which reminds me. How did those Spitfires happen to be up there? They saved our necks."

"They didn't happen," Wilson said. "We asked the Eighth Army for help in keeping the sky clean when the C-47 lands with the new weapon." He looked at his watch. "Almost ten-hundred. Let's get over to the airstrip."

"Us?" Troy said, withdrawing. "Like this? Ordnance and missiles aren't our show. Anyway, you said you couldn't explain us to Washington."

"Maybe I'll have to explain how the targets were selected," Wilson said.

Wilson settled his white varnished helmet with the gold

159

eagle on his head and strapped on his twin pearl handled pistols. For the benefit of the civilian ordnance expert, Troy thought, hiding his smile. The man from Washington was going to wonder what kind of weird company he'd fallen into. Wilson was looking thoughtfully at the Hispano-Suiza when Troy tromped out.

"Let's take the car," he said. "It's a rather impressive vehicle." He opened the back door and sat in the middle. Moffitt sat on one side and Troy on the other. Tully took the steering wheel. Wilson pointed at the gas and water cans and the handbags. "You can clean those things out while we wait."

Troy's heart sank. The car didn't belong to them, but he'd hoped they might be able to conveniently misplace it so it would be available to them when they had a need for it. He had become attached to the big old tub.

Tully stopped at the camouflage net over their hole in the ground and unloaded the cargo from the backseat and the weapons from the front. The C-47 came in as they circled the trucks and parked near the middle of the strip. The aircraft stopped at the end of the runway with reversed props howling and blowing up a sandstorm. It swung about and stopped opposite the car. Wilson indicated the Rat Patrol should tag along and Peilowski ran up to join the welcoming committee. Troy felt ridiculous in his turtleneck sweater and pointed shoes and with the weapons at his belt. Moffitt, in his wrinkled and stained cream-colored gabardine, was no prize. Hitch and Tully were the most unsavory GIs he'd ever seen.

A door near the tail of the C-47 swung back and banged the fuselage. A ladder was dropped and a one-star general in a summer worsted uniform climbed down. Troy started to edge toward the trucks. He was followed by a dumpy civilian in a sweat shirt and baggy slacks. Troy stopped to watch. The two men walked toward Wilson, who took one step forward and waited. Troy wanted to laugh. Wilson and the Rat Patrol were the silliest-looking group in the Army.

The CO saluted the general and nodded to the civilian. "I'm Wilson," he said. "We are pleased to have you here."

The lieutenant general was inspecting Wilson. "Caruthers," he said. "Ordnance." Caruthers had scraggly gray

160

eyebrows and the jaw of an English bulldog. He also had a triple row of ribbons that went back to World War I. He brought up the civilian. He had thick black hair with a monstrous cowlick and black-rimmed glasses that hid most of his face. "Mr. Spain," Caruthers said. "Can you run a couple trucks back to the plane? We have some crates to unload."

"Of course, sir," Wilson said and summoned Peilowski. "Do you want to supervise the unloading, General?"

"What for?" Caruthers snapped. "They're just wooden crates. Shove them in the trucks. Take them to your headquarters and we'll tell you what to do with them."

Peilowski trotted off. Troy backed away. He felt like an extra thumb. "Come on," he growled to Moffitt. "We don't belong here."

The grizzled general found Hitch and Tully, Moffitt and him and the bushy eyebrows went up.

"Oh!" Wilson pointed each of them out. Troy felt like a specimen. "Sergeants Troy and Moffitt. Privates Hitchcock and Pettigrew." He smiled benignly at the Rat Patrol. "Men, General Caruthers. Mr. Spain."

Hitch and Tully saluted. Moffitt and Troy stood at attention. Troy was uncomfortably conscious that he was bareheaded, in civilian clothing and carried an arsenal in his belt. The general confronted them, standing straddle-legged, arms behind his back. His eyes jumped from one to the other.

"Frankly, Colonel," he said, turning to Wilson, "I am curious. Why did you introduce me to these men? Only one is in anything that approaches a uniform. Two are in civilian clothes. They all look like brigands."

"They have just returned from a mission into Jerry's camp," Wilson said with a laugh. "They have charted the enemy's gun positions so that your test firing may be a purposeful demonstration. I have made plans to follow up your bombardment with an offensive against the enemy position."

"Indeed!" Caruthers said in some surprise. "This is gratifying. Splendid. Commendable. Since you have been so cooperative, perhaps you would do one more thing that would be invaluable to us."

"Of course, sir," Wilson said graciously.

"Good," Caruthers said. "I would like your four men to return behind the enemy lines to observe the effectiveness of this new weapon first hand."

"Of course," Wilson said, holding the back door of the Hispano-Suiza open for Caruthers and Spain. He got in beside Spain. Troy looked at Tully and nodded toward the steering wheel. Wilson leaned across Spain to the general. "I want to tell you an amusing little story about what happened last night to the Jerry commander. . . ."

22

Considerably worse mentally than physically for his night in the net, Dietrich had swept his cold lighted tent with his eyes when Grosse opened the door of the staff car. He noted the rent in the back wall, the damp sand of the floor, the cot that looked as if someone had been sleeping on it and his mounting fury threatened to explode. He stepped to the locker, opened it for a bottle of brandy and saw that only one remained. He scowled, swinging to the table where two empty glasses stood. There had been a bottle of American whisky and he distinctly remembered two bottles of brandy in the locker. Removing the last bottle of brandy, he poured himself a stiff drink, tossed it off. He was becoming more wrathful by the moment. Not only had the Sergeants Troy and Moffitt kidnapped him from under the noses of his men, but they had humiliated him in his own camp and while his back was turned, men in his command had presumed to take his liquor and sleep or sit on his cot.

"Grosse!" he roared, and the orderly-driver stepped into the glare of the gas lamp almost at once. His shoulders

162

drooped and his eyes were hapless. He looked as if he were going to snivel. Dietrich felt no compassion.

"What do you know about this?" He swung his arm sharply about to indicate the condition of the tent. "Who has been here?"

"It was the Americans," Grosse mumbled. "It was the Rat Patrol."

"I know that!" Dietrich felt his face burning with rage. "Who was here?" He pointed to the cot, then to the table and locker. "Who drank my liquor?"

"I tried to warn you and could get no further," Grosse said. "I collapsed on the cot. I am sorry, *mein Hauptmann.* I had been attacked by the Sergeant Troy in the back of the tent. I tried to tell you they were the Rat Patrol, but you would not listen."

"Who else was here?" Dietrich thundered. "Did you drink the liquor?"

"No, *Herr Hauptmann,* I did not drink the liquor."

"Who was it, Grosse? Doeppler?" Dietrich watched Grosse furiously but closely.

"It was Doeppler," Grosse admitted miserably.

"Get Doeppler," Dietrich fumed. "Send him to me at once."

"*Ja, mein Hauptmann,*" Grosse said and turned and ran.

Dietrich sat behind his table with the brandy bottle and a single glass in plain sight. When Doeppler reported, his back no longer was so stiff as it had been the day before and his eyes were red-rimmed. They jumped to the bottle and Dietrich thought the lieutenant's haggard face paled. Doeppler clicked his heels and braced his shoulders. Dietrich took his time, pouring the brandy deliberately. He sipped and studied the lieutenant with eyes he himself could feel turning from hot rage to cold wrath.

"Was it you, Doeppler, who removed a bottle of brandy from my locker?" Dietrich asked at last and gritted his teeth.

"*Ja, Herr Hauptmann,*" Doeppler said, snapping his jaw like a puppet.

"Did it occur to you that you were stealing my property?" Dietrich asked savagely. "That I could and should have you shot?"

"*Herr Hauptmann,*" Doeppler said desperately. "I

163

removed it thinking only that it would be handy to revive you when we had rescued you."

"Rescue!" Dietrich exploded. "How can you call that farce you permitted a rescue? I do not recall your offering a drink of brandy to me when I had need of it. All you did was engage in staring like a dumb ox."

"Ja, Herr Hauptmann." Doeppler was at it again, looking at tne tent wall above Dietrich's head.

"Where is the bottle now?" Dietrich demanded.

"I am sorry, *herr Hauptmann,* but I was shaken by the tragic misofrtune and felt the need for revival myself," Doeppler said.

"The entire bottle?"

"Ja, mein Hauptmann."

"Doeppler, if you had drunk the entire bottle, you would be flat on your face in the sand." Dietrich examined the man with distaste. "I am not yet through with this theft from your commanding officer. There are other matters, however, which must come first. Do you have the list of men I ordered you to prepare?"

Doeppler reached inside his rumpled and soiled coat and handed Dietrich a page from a notebook on which the names of six men had been written in a shaky hand.

"I do not see the name of Grosse," Dietrich accused.

"I thought you were aware that he was present," Doeppler said stolidly. "He drove you to the camp."

"Nor also do I see the name of Lieutenant Doeppler," Dietrich said. "Every man, I commanded." He handed the paper back to Doeppler. "Add them now."

Doeppler found a fountain pen, managed to unscrew the cap and write the names. His hands had begun to tremble so badly that he had to press his elbows to his ribs to join the pen together.

"Now," Dietrich said, feeling calmer than he had. He sipped a little brandy. "You will take the men on this list into the Allied camp at once, before it is light, and destroy the British twenty-five-pounder with charges."

Doeppler looked at Dietrich aghast. "Including Grosse?" he asked when he was able to speak.

"Including Grosse," Dietrich said. "You know where the gun is—in the camouflaged pit. How you carry out the mission is up to you. That is all."

Doeppler saluted mechanically, turned and tottered from the tent. Dietrich found a few crackers and a piece of cheese Grosse had overlooked, poured another glass of brandy and shouted for Kloake, the radio operator.

"Kloake, contact headquarters of the Afrika Korps," Dietrich said.

"At this hour?" the boy gasped and his blue eyes widened.

"Call me as soon as you have the Field Marshal," Dietrich said. "I will speak to him in person."

Dietrich went over his plans as he removed boots and tunic and lay under a blanket on his cot. He would ask for three Messerschmitts to follow the route over the ridge Sergeants Troy and Moffitt must have taken. That would eliminate them. He realized that he should not allow his ire to influence his judgment on military affairs, but this time he was determined to remove the entire Rat Patrol. With the twenty-five-pounder blown up, Dietrich was ready to send his strengthened column roaring down from the heights to ravage the Allied camp in the morning. Never in his life had he been subjected to such indignity as he had endured at the hands of the Rat Patrol this day.

Doeppler's legs and shoulders ached and there were tender places in his bones. He stumbled down the grade with his little squad and they were sullen as they groped with their feet on the decline in the blackness before the first gray light of dawn. At least, he thought wretchedly, he'd been able to shut off the flares and silence the guns for a few hours so the only danger they'd have to worry about was the enemy. They carried machine pistols, grenades and plastic charges. They were going to immobilize the British gun about which the Arab had sold information. They'd do it at all costs, Doeppler thought grimly. Perhaps when this duty was done, he'd be able to get some rest.

When Doeppler reached the desert beyond the foot of the slope, he turned south away from the grade. It was the route the three false Enna brothers had taken earlier and he wondered how one of them had been able to slip back onto the ridge. He circled wide about the area where he knew the tanks and halftracks were stationed, reasoning that there would be guards about and crews would be in the slit trenches. When the squad had worked back to the lines of trucks that stood between the camouflaged pit and the airstrip, they went to their hands and knees, pushing their pistols ahead, squirming through the sand in the chill.

Despite the fatigue that even stretched his face stiff, Doeppler could not help smiling now at the thought of Dietrich flopping in the net. Doeppler realized his squad and he were being punished because the Rat Patrol had made Dietrich ridiculous. The Rat Patrol had roamed the camp at will, finding targets for the twenty-five-pounder. Doubtful as it seemed, perhaps Doeppler could reclaim some measure of esteem by carrying out this mission successfully.

Doeppler grasped the arm of Grosse and held the squad flat under a truck as the squishy tread of a sentry's desert boots moved past just beyond the wheels. It was the first guard who'd approached and Doeppler clung motionless to the ground. It was cold and he was afraid his teeth would chatter. Someone behind him sniffled. The guard turned and walked rapidly back toward the truck. He hesitated and disappeared in the dark alley between the lines of trucks toward the airstrip. In a moment Doeppler heard him calling softly and a second voice answered. A third joined in.

Although Doeppler did not understand what they were saying, he did comprehend 'Arab' and 'shoot.' He felt himself go warm as the perspiration burst out on his forehead, and then he turned cold. The three guards walked slowly down the lines of trucks, pausing every few steps to listen. They moved toward the pit.

"Grosse," he whispered. "I'll try to go in alone. There's no chance for all of us. If I don't make it, try a rush with the others."

He snaked from under one truck to the next, pausing every few feet, counting the vehicles to make his way back. The three guards approached again and he waited until they were by. When he could no longer hear them, he crawled from the front line of trucks and ran straight ahead. The pit as he remembered it was about two hundred yards beyond the trucks. He counted again as he ran and when he'd taken two hundred paces, knelt and began to feel the sand. A few yards to the right and his hand touched

166

coarse netting. He lay for several minutes, listening for the guards to return or the men in the pit to stir. He thought he detected a faint aroma of coffee and the lingering smell of cigarettes. He was tempted to throw a grenade and run but he was afraid he might not demolish the weapon unless he placed a charge at some vital position.

He lifted the net and moved down a sand ramp gently, a few inches at a time. He thought he heard the breathing of someone inside. He lay perfectly still for several minutes and the man snored gently. He went on again and his face was wet with perspiration when he reached the floor of the pit. He now could hear the breathing of a second person and he smelled gasoline and oil. When he could determine the positions of the two men, he crept ahead until he bumped into a vehicle. Quickly running his hand over the front of the car, he recognized it as a jeep. He backed away from it toward the other side of the pit and discovered a second jeep.

Doeppler was puzzled. The two jeeps of the Rat Patrol were parked under the net and the two sleeping men must be the men who drove them. It did not seem like a gun position nor a gun crew to him. Working his way between the second jeep and the side of the pit, he determined there was nothing else in that space. Backing out, he wriggled under the jeep and lay quietly until he again was certain that one man slept near the front and the other near the back of the hollow. Gently he urged his way out until he lay on the sand in the middle of the hole in the desert between the two men. He found no gun mount.

There was nothing in the pit but two jeeps and two men. The Arabs had sold false information to Dietrich. He almost smiled until he remembered where he was and quickly started edging back around the jeep toward the ramp. One of the men stirred and muttered something. Doeppler clutched the ground. He let several minutes crawl by before he went on again, up and out from under the net.

When he was satisfied no guard was walking toward him, he retraced the route he had taken to the truck and went back under them. A guard moved by and into the silence. Doeppler went on until a hand grasped his arm.

"Move out," Doeppler whispered urgently.

Bodies scraped through the sand and the squad crept out

the way they had come in. Well south of the truc...
risked getting to his knees, looking quickly all aroun...
sky was getting lighter and the hulking tanks and hal...
were visible in outline.

"What happened?" someone asked.

"No gun, just jeeps and men in there," Doepple...
"We'd better move fast."

Although the dangerous part of the mission was...
the men still were sullen as they moved quickly acro...
desert flat. They started to trot when they reache...
grade, although it seemed to Doeppler that his legs w...
rubbery he would surely lost his footing. At the rid...
dismissed the squad and walked to Dietrich's tent. I...
clear, pale daylight now.

A guard halted him as he neared Dietrich's tent.

"It's all right," Doeppler said. His throat ached wit...
effort of speaking. "Lieutenant Doeppler reporting to...
tain Dietrich from a mission."

The guard pointed to Doeppler's weapon and explos...
"You'll have to leave them behind. I will say who is he...

When Doeppler stepped into the tent, Dietrich was...
ting on the edge of his cot in breeches and shirt. His...
was lined harshly with sleeplessness and his eyes were l...
and dark. "Well, Doeppler," he said. "No earth shal...
explosion lifted me from my cot. I have been lying l...
awake, listening for it. What excuse have you for y...
failure this time?"

"No excuse, *Herr Hauptmann*," Doeppler said stiffly...
did not fail. There is no gun. The Arab lied."

Dietrich leaped from the cot and stood in the sand in...
stocking feet. His eyes blazed. "Are you certain? This c...
not be so. What was in the pit?"

"Two jeeps only and two men asleep," Doeppler said...
myself investigated."

"You disposed of the men and left charges in the jee...
of course," Dietrich stated.

"No," Doeppler said proudly. "I realized that wou...
alert the enemy we had been in his camp. The Rat Pat...
knew we had been informed the Allies possessed a lon...
range gun. I reasoned that as long as they believed v...
thought the information we had purchased to be true, the...
would be careless. It is an opportunity to surprise them."

"Doeppler, you fool," Dietrich said furiously. "Those were two members of the Rat Patrol asleep. You should have disposed of them at any cost. You have allowed yourself to be outwitted again. The Rat Patrol, alive, know our positions. We are going to attack and you have weakened us. Even the lying Arab outwitted you. Now you can take your useless squad and find the Arab so he can be punished. At once. Do not return until you have captured him."

23

The Hispano-Suiza threw a hot shower of dust over Troy, Moffitt and Hitch who stood at the edge of the airstrip while Tully drove the general, the colonel and the civilian to HQ.

"There goes the last of that car," Troy said wryly and wiped his forehead on his arm.

"It may be the last of the Rat Patrol if the general sends us back behind the Jerry lines to observe the fire," Hitch said and reached into his pocket for a stick of bubble gum. "We're stuck with these disguises until they send some stuff to get them off. All Dietrich has to do is catch sight of us and we've had it."

"I'm curious about the crates," Moffitt said. "Shall we pop over?"

Troy glanced once toward the ridge. He didn't have his field glasses in his turtleneck attire, but he imagined he could see Dietrich standing on a rock with his binoculars focused on the airstrip and wondering what and who was on the C-47. He turned with the others toward the trucks. Troy resented the casual, almost breezy way this new mission had been given. The only way he knew they could attempt to return was over the mined back trail and his hands and knees were scratched and sore from the clambering he'd done the night before.

Large wooden crates were being lowered from the belly of the C-47 and swung into waiting trucks. Each crate filled a truck. There were twelve of them and nine seemed relatively heavy while the other three were comparatively light. The trucks rumbled in the direction of the HQ tent. Puzzled, Troy turned to Moffitt and Hitch. They both lifted their hands in bewilderment.

Back at the rathole, Troy and Moffitt washed and changed into familiar clothes and hats. Tully did not return for another ten minutes and when he did he was scowling.

"Where's the car?" Hitch asked.

"Parked behind the trucks," Tully said. "The CO wants us at HQ."

"What for?" Troy asked suspiciously.

"He didn't say," Tully said, "but I think it has something to do with the job he took for us."

Troy pulled back and bumped into Moffitt as soon as he started into the tent. Wilson with General Caruthers and Mr. Spain were seated at the table in the stifling place and half a dozen tank officers were crowded on two cots. Peilowski seemed to have been crowded out. A strange wooden contraption, apparently a model, was on the table in front of Spain.

"Crowd in," Wilson said good-naturedly. "It's a briefing."

Spain stood. He seemed insignificant and uncomfortable in his large dark-rimmed glasses and baggy sweat shirt. He cleared his throat and the eyes that were turned to him were more curious than interested. His voice, however, was resonant and commanding.

"Gentlemen," he said, "this is a model of a rocket launcher."

Troy inspected the model quickly. He had seen rocket launchers before. This seemed to have an unusual number of tubes and was constructed at an odd cant.

"The rocket launcher," Spain went on, "consists of sixty tubes constructed of plywood. It is designed to be mounted on the turret of a Sherman tank."

170

The men on the cots wiped the moisture from their foreheads and leaned forward. Troy could feel a prickle of excitement.

"All sixty projectiles can be launched in thirty seconds," Spain said. "The weapon launches thirty-eight-pound missiles which strike with the destructive effect of 105 mm. shells at forty-four hundred yards."

Troy felt a quick stir run through the tent.

"How many launchers will be tested?" Wilson turned to Spain and asked.

General Caruthers answered. "We have brought three launchers. Each will fire three rounds of sixty missiles. They will be pulled off-target for reloading and the firing will be staggered from three tanks. The test will give us the effect of five hundred and forty 105mm. shells with which to saturate the area."

"What area or areas will be the targets?" a bareheaded, red-faced tank commander asked.

Wilson glanced at charts before him. "We have pinpointed weapons positions on either side of the grade beginning with the mortars and including the rocket launchers, antitank guns and 75 mm. cannon. The grade is their safe passage. We expect the missiles to have a psychological shock effect. Our armor will proceed up the grade immediately with the firing of the final group of missiles. Our armor is prepared for the tank. Zero hour will be thirteen-thirty." He looked at three lieutenants seated together on one cot. "Byrd, Hipple, Furfal, you will command the Shermans on which the launchers will be mounted. Stations for launching and reloading will be assigned. I believe that is all. Good luck."

Troy stepped from the tent into the blazing sun with Moffitt, Hitch and Tully as the officers walked briskly out. Dietrich was in for a surprise, he thought. The Jerry captain expected a single 25-pounder but he was going to be smashed with a crushing bombardment. When only Caruthers, Wilson and Spain remained in the tent, still talking at the table, Troy stepped in.

"Excuse me, sir," he said to General Caruthers. "If we're going to get behind the Jerry lines, we'd better get started. Do you have any instructions?"

"If you leave at zero hour, you will have ample time,"

171

the general said. His jaw jutted when he smiled.

"I don't know what you mean," Troy said bluntly.

"When I said behind the lines I didn't say on the ground," the general said. "You will accompany me in the aircraft. I want to see whether we have a good pattern and five pairs of eyes are better than one."

"Whew," Troy said, saluted and left.

A hastily improvised tent of canvas and camouflage netting had been erected between the HQ tent and the pit, and the trucks driven there to unload. The desert flat was being bombed with smoke and the white clouds concealed the three tanks that clattered from their positions to line up behind the workshop. The Vs of tanks and halftracks were closing formation. Smoke bombs continued to haze the valley. The ridge became nervous with what could not be observed and the 75s began to throw shells that fell out of range in the smoke.

The Rat Patrol halted at the side and watched as the sweating crews swarmed over the hot steel tanks, installing the strange banks of plywood cylinders on the turrets. The launchers consisted of four rows of fifteen tubes banked at slants. As each Sherman was fitted and loaded, it rolled from the tent and followed an ammunition truck which had been assigned it.

The crew was working on the third Sherman when Peilowski panted into the baking workshop. Tendrils of smoke seemed to stream after him. "Enemy column starting down the grade," he shouted.

"Let's go," Caruthers snapped and turned toward the airstrip. He beckoned Troy, setting out at a dead trot.

Troy glimpsed Wilson slamming into the staff car and reaching for the transceiver. He must have called the C-47 first because the propellers were turning when the Rat Patrol followed the general onto the strip. The aircraft was shaking and roaring by the time they climbed into the belly. The door banged and the ship gunned down the runway. The general headed through the cargo compartment to six bucket seats that had been placed forward and the plane was airborne.

The aircraft circled to the west. Below, a puffy haze covered much of the flat, but as Troy watched, an awkward-appearing Sherman broke into the clear and headed toward

172

the grade. It was supported by two Shermans which had not been equipped with launchers. The Jerry armor was about halfway down the grade and both the Shermans and Mark IVs were traveling at about the same rate of speed. It appeared the three Shermans would meet the entire Jerry force near the bottom of the slope, but abruptly the missile cluster on the Sherman puffed and the rocket soared dead into the leading tanks. Smoke erupted along the grade and the column ground to a halt. The first launcher-equipped Sherman already was scooting back to rendezvous when the entire ridge and slope spit smoke and fire. It was difficult to see the lower part of the grade, but it was tangled confusion near the top.

The aircraft circled away from the guns on the ridge and came back over the flat. A second launcher had moved up toward the grade and Troy had a glimpse of the missiles piercing the haze and breaking into the center of the Jerry column. The whole slope was draped with dusty haze through which orange fire licked now and then. At the top of the ridge, tanks and halftracks looked like scuttling beetles as they tried to maneuver away from the safe passage.

The third launcher was in place now and threw its sixty missiles on the crest into the retreating armor. Before they were drowned in the smoke, tiny dark figures scurried from gun positions. The smoke had cleared from some of the flat and two Vs were waiting to rush the ridge. Wilson never will get around the wreckage piled on the slope, Troy thought as a Sherman appeared with another load of missiles. This cluster was directed into the base of the slope beyond the flat and it seemed half the hill went up in the combined explosions of mines and rockets. The launchers concentrated bombardment now at the side of the grade and when their last loads had spurted from the tubes, they were jettisoned and the tanks pushed up through the swirling clouds. The rest of Wilson's column ran after them.

The aircraft circled the ridge and General Caruthers leaned forward toward Troy. "Where?" he shouted above the pounding of the engines.

Troy leaned across to point the coastal highway. The route leading to it was marked with crawling armor and running figures. The flight that had been interrupted by the

173

position on the ridge had started and Wilson's column emerged triumphant on the ridge. To the east some of the supply trucks had begun to move out.

"Magnificent!" the general shouted. He was grinning.

Troy, Moffitt, Hitch and Tully all grinned back at him.

Caruthers stepped into the pilot's compartment and when he returned, the C-47 turned back over the flat and thundered in for a landing at the strip. Wilson might send a flying squad of Shermans in pursuit of Dietrich, but Troy knew he would have to pause at the commanding and strategic ridge position to clear the slope and consolidate the gains from the battle he had won. Beyond, to the west, the territory was still controlled by the Jerries. Dietrich would probably limp somewhere to the safety of the Afrika Korps and fight another day again.

The pilot came from his compartment before the Rat Patrol had followed General Caruthers from the C-47. A broad smile lighted his tanned face as he nodded and said, "You fellows are an odd lot to keep the general company. Any of you speak English?"

"Burione," Hitch said with a fierce scowl.

"We're spotters," Troy said with a grin.

"Oh?" the pilot said, seeming surprised. "You happen to spot that funny little Jerry car that was heading south, away from the road the others were taking? It was weaving all over the desert. Either the driver was drunk or chasing something."

"Oh?" Troy said, interested.

"Yeah," the pilot said, shaking his head. "Sure was funny. Everybody else going northwest and this one car going south. Wasn't anything I could see in that direction."

Troy lifted his eyebrows at Moffitt. The Englishman's mustache bristled but his eyes gleamed. Troy looked at Hitch and Moffitt. Their heads bobbed in unison.

"Let's shake it," Troy said and jumped to the ground.

The four of them ran to the camouflaged pit. While Moffitt and Troy jerked away the net, Hitch and Tully started the jeeps and ran them out. They hastily checked weapons and ammunition, cans of gas and water. The jeeps spun in the loose sand and raced toward the HQ net. General Caruthers popped out his grizzled head.

174

"What's up?" he shouted.

Hitch and Tully braked and Troy said, "Going to find out why a Jerry patrol car was heading in the opposite direction from the retreating column."

"Room for a passenger?" the general called and without waiting for an answer slid in the front seat of Troy's jeep beside Hitch.

Side by side the heavily armed little vehicles sped across the desert flat and lunged to the chewed-up side of the grade. The smoke rose from the smashed and blasted Jerry armor and from the craters. They wove through confused Allied and Jerry armor, past Dietrich's tent where Wilson already was setting up HQ. He stood in the entrance in his white varnished helmet, lifted a hand in confusion and stared after them as Caruthers returned the casual greeting.

The jeeps bounded down the rocky slope that led to the coastal highway and turned west on it. Troy picked up a submachine gun and handed it to the general. Moffitt and Troy both were at the spade handles of their .50 caliber Brownings, but the sand and stone that burned on either side of the road seemed deserted. The sun beat at Troy and the wind slashed at his face. Even with the mustache and black hair under the bush hat, he felt normal again.

When Hitch and Tully swerved the jeeps off the road and started south over hard baked clay toward the rocky desert sand beyond, Caruthers turned his head to Troy.

"If there's shooting I want to be in it," he called. "But only for today. I have appointments in Washington day after tomorrow."

They were off the hardpack and into the sand when Troy saw a dust streamer curling in the distance. Tully's jeep surged ahead almost at the same moment Hitch's dropped back. The general swung about and glared at Troy.

"You're trigger-happy," Troy called. "I don't think there'll be any shooting."

Three men were in the Volkswagen patrol car, one at the steering wheel and two in the back seat. One of the men in the rear wore a white robe. Tully drew alongside and Moffitt leaned toward the other car over his machine gun. Hitch parked behind and Troy saw the driver who had his hands in the air and was shouting at Moffitt in German was the officer, Doeppler, from Dietrich's camp. The Jerry in the back was Dietrich's orderly-driver, Grosse. The third man was an Arab.

Moffitt turned. His mustache was lifted in a J. Enna smile. "He said they were coming over the ridge to bargain," he called. "They captured the deceitful Arab and will turn him over to us if we don't send them back to Dietrich."

"What a way to run a war," General Caruthers growled and shoved his tommy gun to the floor.